KING

Jimmy DaSaint

KING

**Published by DASAINT ENTERTAINMENT
Po Box 97 Bala Cynwyd, PA 19004
Website: www.dasaintentertainment.com**

"A noble King will rule his empire and protect his loved ones. He will also raise his sword and fight with his soldiers in war."
— **Jimmy DaSaint**

Keep your head up to all my brothers inside of the cage.
They want to break us, then watch us boil with inner rage.

Keep your head up to all my soldiers behind the wall.
They're out to destroy our race and humiliate us when we attempt to stand tall.

They are out to kill us off with man-made diseases, homosexuality, and prison.

They've replaced our real names with numbers and our minds with false religions.

Keep your head up Bosses, Kings, Queens, and Leaders!
Let's remove the strings from the puppet masters and stop letting them deceive us.

It's time to educate ourselves and put the foolishness far away.

It's time to be the Kings and Queens you were born to be and it starts with you Today!

-Jimmy DaSaint

"Oh, let the wickedness of the wicked come to an end; but establish the just: For the righteous God tests the hearts and minds.

-Psalms 7:9

I
ATLANTIC CITY

Inside a private suite at the Harrah's Casino, Darrius "King" Smith stood at the table listening to his notorious cousin, Face, as he dropped some crucial knowledge and advice about the ruthless drug game. Norman "Face" Smith Jr., was once the biggest drug lord in America. He was the only Kingpin to beat the U.S. Government at trial, and he retained all his wealth in the process. In the eyes of many, Face, was a living legend. His power was limitless, and his reach was impressive; The President of the United States was only a phone call away.

"When you build your crew, everyone must have complete trust in you and their loyalty can never be questioned. Any doubt they can't commit to what needs to be done and accomplish your vision, terminate your losses. Your woman must be your strength when you're weak and even when you're up. Your right-hand man should be willing to kill and die for you without a second thought. Your men should never look down on you. In their eyes, you should always shine like the brightest star in God's universe. Never speak to the law. Never speak harsh words about others, not even your enemies. Make your moves in silence but leave a powerful impact. Always be prepared and willing to face the biggest obstacles in your life, and learn to accept death. Never fear it because it's a debt we all must pay; some sooner than others. Learn, listen and hear more so you can learn. Watch more than you speak and only speak when you must. The wiser you are the most successful you will become."

King nodded his head in agreement. He was in awe just being in the presence of his cousin, and he appreciated being served some firsthand knowledge. His older cousin, Face, has always been his mentor and idol. Each word spoken was taken serious and retained in memory.

When Face had finished talking, he stood up from his chair and walked around the long wooden, glazed table towards his cousin. He stared directly into King's keen brown eyes and said, "Be the King that you were born to be because the torch has been passed. Now you're the head of a growing hundred million dollar a year empire, and there's no turning back. Are you ready?"

Face didn't take his surveying eyes off of his younger cousin. He waited to hear the words that would reassure him this young man's heart was ready for the challenges that would surely be awaiting him upon his acceptance. As he cleared his throat, King vehemently said, "Yes, I'm ready," as he sternly shook Face's right hand.

Face smiled as he looked at their hands. He was impressed with his cousin's firm grip. Face gave King a brief hug before he straightened his tie, glanced at himself in the mirror and then left the suite.

Moments later King walked out of the suite and went down to the lobby. He watched as Face got into an all-black tinted Mercedes-Benz and pulled off. King then walked into the bar and sat down at an empty table. Minutes later a tall, dark-skinned man walked over and began to sit down beside him.

Quincy was Face's right-hand man, and he had a message for the newly crowned young boss.

"This is your access card into the warehouse," Quincy said, as he sat down and passed Face a small card. "Everything you need will be there, untraceable phones, weapons and, of course, the product. Your supplier will contact you and give you the rest of the information you'll need," he continued. "I got it, is that it Q," King asked, as they stood up from the table.

Quincy put his mouth to King's ear and whispered, "A man was watching your every move." King was perplexed because he hadn't seen anyone. He began to scan the area for any strangers who might have been eyeing him. "Where is he," King asked. Quincy smiled and quietly said, "He's slumped over the wheel of his car in the parking lot," and then he walked out of the bar area. King didn't know what to say as he sat back down.

For the next half hour, King sat at the table in deep thought. He was disappointed with himself because he hadn't been alert and knew he needed to be on point going forward. The watching eyes were all around him, and his enemies had faces that he hadn't even seen.

King picked up his phone and tried to reach his friend, Rome. Rome had driven King to Atlantic City, but now that he was calling him he couldn't get him on the phone. King assumed he was gambling in one of the casinos or kicking it with a girl, so he went upstairs to his room.

As King lay back on his king-sized bed, the thoughts of the current day ran through his mind. He had taken on a new and dangerous position, and not even twenty-four hours had passed before a body count had started. His thoughts were frequent, plenty and exhausting. The young king lay his slim, but athletic, physique deep into the comforting bed; resting his mind and body.

11
EARLY THE NEXT MORNING

As the bright rays of yellow sun shined through the window, King was awakened from his deep, peaceful sleep. The three-day business and leisure trip to Atlantic City was needed. King grabbed his cellphone and yet again called his friend Rome. Still there was no answer.

After taking a warm, steam filled shower and getting dressed, King left his private suite to find his friend. He continued to call Rome's phone but each time he got the same response, none. King walked around the entire casino and pool area, but he couldn't find him. Rome was King's childhood friend, and when King said he needed a ride to AC, Rome was down to drive. He offered to take King to Atlantic City. The secret meeting he shared with his cousin, Face, was something he hadn't mentioned to anyone. Now it was all too strange, and clearly not a coincidence that his friend was nowhere to be found.

King continued to search for his friend. As he made his way back around to the lobby, he saw several cop cars in the parking lot through the glass entrance doors. King cautiously walked outside to survey the area and to understand why more cop cars continued to arrive. As he got closer, he was in shock. He had to remind himself to keep his cool even though his eyes wanted to jump out of their sockets because of what they were observing. Rome lay slumped over the wheel of his car. "Damn," King mumbled under his breath.

King rushed back into the casino. He knew Quincy had murdered his friend, but it had to be a mistake. He pressed the elevator button and entered as he waited for his designated floor. Rome was his friend. Quincy had made a move without consulting King, and now his mistake had left his friend dead.

Once on the fifth floor, he exited and made his way to Quincy's suite. "I don't believe this shit," King said knocking on the door. "We need to talk," King said, as he hurriedly made his way into Quincy's room. Quincy was cool as he watched King rush inside. After he closed the door and locked it, he walked over to King, whose face was filled with confusion, anger, and sadness.

"You killed my friend Rome Quincy! You murdered the wrong man," King shouted. As calm as a monk, Quincy placed his arm on King's tense right shoulder, and looked into his eyes and said, "Your friend is a rat. He's an informant for the DEA." King was confused. "Rome? DEA? He's been my friend since high school," King said. "Are you finished," Quincy asked. "Yeah, I'm finished," King replied, with added bass to his voice. "Your friend Jarome Davis also known as Rome was arrested three weeks ago by FBI and DEA agents on the intent to distribute two kilos of crack cocaine. And don't be silly enough to ask me how I know. Now is one of those times when you just listen." King knew he needed to listen to Quincy's words.

"Rome was working with Philly's drug titan, Vance Lewis, your competitor and chief rival. The FEDS have; well had been using Rome as a street informer to gather info on some major drug camps. Instead of snitching on his boss he was tailing you so he could set you up.

And just to clear your mind, know that your cousin has friends all over. A call came in from our sources and verified exactly what Rome was plotting. Once we knew, we did what we needed. This is the business you're in. When it's time to act, you move."

Quincy walked over to the dresser and pulled out a small microphone with a long wire attached.

"This was taped to his chest. He was recording everything," Quincy said. King sat down in the chair and shook his head. How could he have been so blind, he thought to himself? He was in a position of power and his inability to recognize the face of his enemy had him fuming. He had fucked up. Thank God for his cousin and his watching eyes or his reign would have never begun, he thought.

"Don't let it stress you King, but don't let it happen again. Your circles got to be tighter because the next time could be your last. Everyone ain't no friend no matter how long you've known them or what school Y'all attended. Keep them eyes open at all times and stay ahead of your enemy." "You're right man. Damn, Rome was working for Vance and the FEDS." "Yeah, but the good news is things got handled. But Face ain't always gonna be around. You've gotta start having your own back. You have to look out for your whole crew, and you can't do that if their biggest asset is behind bars or eating dirt. So be on point round the clock because ain't no days off in this game. One mistake and your entire empire crumbles."

King listened as Quincy's words sank into his soul. Today he had learned a major lesson. He took the shame he felt and promised himself he'd never have to take this test again. His eyes were open. Everyone would be studied and kept at a distance until he knew who they were and what motives they had.

III
LATER THAT NIGHT

Inside a small row house in North Philly, King was surrounded by the members of his crew. Six-footer Haze, Zark, Chino (his godbrother), Trouble, Nas-his 6'5 husky personal bodyguard, and his secret weapon, Zeta; a beautiful, tall redbone with a flawless face and superior toned body.

King observed the room and his expression showed extreme seriousness as thoughts ran through his mind. The meeting with Face has been at the forefront of his thoughts, and he'd never let that knowledge leave him. After a few deep breaths, he was ready to begin, but he realized someone was missing.

"Where the hell is Biggie," he asked. "I told him to be on time but you know Biggie's always late," Haze replied. King's patience was wearing thin but before he could respond Biggie, standing at only 4'2, but stocky, with his rough dark skin pushed opened the door. King and Biggie had been best friends since Kindergarten, and although Biggie was small in stature, he was no pushover. He grew up tough, and his heart was cold. His blood was filled with the lineage of killers, and on the streets of Philly, he was well known to put one in you quick.

"Where you been at man," King asked. "Taking care of some important business but wassup with all these serious ass faces," he asked, climbing into a chair and sitting down. "I had a meeting yesterday and got some disturbing news," King said. "What's wrong," Zeta asked instantly becoming worried. "Rome is dead." "What! Are you serious," Trouble asked. "Yes, as serious as he is dead," King snapped.

King was quiet as he begin pacing around the room, watching every member of his crew. He stared each one up and down but said nothing. He continued to eye them as he walked back and forth.

"Rome was a rat! He was working with the FEDS," King said suddenly. "A rat," Biggie shouted. "Are you serious, Biggie continued. "Yeah, a rat that planned to take us all down. He was working with Vance and his crew too, so only God knows what that nigga had in store for us," King said. "Damn! That no good as nigga," Biggie barked. "Didn't Y'all used to ball together," Haze asked. "Thought you was tight with main-man," he continued. "Yeah back in high school at Gratz, but people change real quick when the FEDS get a hold of them. Loyalty in this game is faded. Nothing's left but greed, envy, and saving your own ass," King said.

His crew looked at him as they thought about his truth filled words. The code in the streets was constantly changing. Each day a new Rat was made. Longtime friendships quickly ended when money was on the line, and one would simply shoot the other in the head. The game was grimy, but it was a game this crew loved. They were all deep in and maybe the last of a dying breed. They had each other's backs. They wanted to reach the top, but as a family; headed by the KING.

IV

After the meeting, everyone received their orders from King and headed out. Biggie was the only one who stayed behind with King. He knew his best friend better than anyone else. Ever since they were five years old, Biggie could tell when something was bothering King. Together they had been through it all and through it all they always had each other's back; no matter the situations or the consequences. The two held no secrets from one another, and King always viewed Biggie as a brother.

"Everything is gonna be cool man, you never told Rome shit, and now that rat is dead," Biggie assured him. "I know but I let someone get close to me that could have brought me down, and it don't sit right. I was sloppy, and I missed all the signs. I feel like a fucking amateur, like a damn fool. I'm getting passed the torch, but I wasn't even ready. I don't know if I can fill his shoes, man. Not making major mistakes like that. I could have brought us all down!"

Biggie climbed down from his chair and walked over to King. "Homey you ain't Face. You will never be. You can't fill his shoes, but you can create and walk in your own, down your path, right," Biggie said. "Yeah, you right," King said. "We all just need to be on point. Your cousin was there this time, but now we've got to be on our game. Face has had your back since you were born, riding hard with you. There for you when you were ballin in college and every other time you needed him. We men now and it's time to man up and do what we were groomed to do."

King nodded in agreement and said, "Truthfully I don't think he ever wanted any of this for me. He always had the same dream I did, that I was going to make it into the NBA. But when I messed my knee up that dream died for both of us." The NBA wasn't in the cards for you, or me," Biggie said as the pair started to laugh. "On a serious note, we gotta keep our circle small and keep our heads in this game. We on another level and I'm focused on the future now. I've got to put this mistake behind me and live by my name. I'm a King and from this moment on I'm going to be nothing less."

V

"So where you going tonight," King asked, as he walked out the back door with Biggie. "I have some important business to take care off. Some shit needs fixing," Biggie answered with a smirk. "You always got some important business to handle. Just be safe and get up with me in the morning," King said.

Biggie watched as King walked over and got into his new BMW. As soon as King drove off a navy-blue Range Rover, driven by his bodyguard, Nas, followed behind closely. Biggie opened the door to his Audi A8 and climbed inside. The car had been customized with over ten-thousand in upgrades to support his small stature. With the added features driving the car was no problem. Biggie turned on his car and the sounds of Drake blazed through his speakers. He then opened up a secret compartment under his seat and took out his favorite toy; a fully loaded Glock 17. He securely placed the gun on his lap and pulled off down the dark street. Tonight someone would pay for violating the code of the streets.

DELAWARE AVENUE

The silver Porsche pulled up and parked in the parking lot of Onyx Gentleman's Club. Inside of the vehicle, Zeta sat patiently waiting. Thirty minutes later a short, attractive brown skinned woman walked out carrying a large Adidas bag. It was Tasty, her girlfriend of three years. Tasty got into the car and before words were exchanged the two greeted one another with a heated, juicy kiss.

"You good Boo," Zeta asked. "Yeah, I'm okay but tonight was slow. All them niggas in there today was thirsty and broke," Tasty said. "It's going to be okay. I told you I have plans for us," Zeta assured her sexy girlfriend. "Well when? I'm ready to retire now. I'm almost twenty-nine, and this stripper life has worn me out. I've had enough," she said. Zeta looked at her girlfriend and then she began to pull off.

"I told you it's important for you to work in the club right now. That's where all the ballers, hustlers and wannabes go. One day your job is going to come in handy. So don't trip about the money, you know you good. I got you covered Boo. Just keep playing your position until you-know-who comes in there." Tasty smiled and then asked, "But what if he or his crew never comes in there?" Confidently Zeta looked at her girlfriend as they sat at the red light and said, "They will. All thirsty niggas do eventually."

Twenty minutes later the car pulled in front of Zeta's loft, located in the quiet Manayunk section of Philly. When they walked in an older Latin woman was sitting on the couch. "Zack is sound asleep in his bedroom," the woman said to Tasty with a thick accent. "Thanks, Maria, I'll see you tomorrow," she said, as the babysitter made her way out of the door.

When the two women were alone, they made their way to the bathroom. Each undressed one another, and when their beautiful, fit, sexy bodies were exposed, they cut the shower on and made their way into the steamy waters. As the water touched their bodies, each was turned on more as they kissed and fingered one another. Zeta went down on her knees. The warm water rained on top of her head as she began to give Tasty a treat of her own.

18ᵀᴴ & ERIE
NORTH PHILLY

For the past hour, Biggie sat inside of his car, which was parked across the street from a corner house. He knew the neighborhood like the back of his hand. He also knew everything about the house he was stalking, and the people who lived inside.

Biggie was a man who enjoyed doing his dirt alone. The only person he trusted besides himself was King, but he never called on him unless it was necessary.

After exiting his car, he placed on his black face mask and walked towards the alley; clutching his loaded Glock that fits securely in the palm of his hand. Like a ghost in the night, he crept through the alley without being seen or heard by anyone. When he approached the back door of the residence, he took out a small screwdriver and started maneuvering the lock. The goal was to get the locked door open without anyone knowing you were trying to gain entry; a goal he had accomplished many times before. When King and Biggie were younger they had their shares of breaking and entering, and each time Biggie was the one handling the locks.

With just a few attempts the door was now open, and as quiet as he could, Biggie eased his way into the house. The lights were out but even in the dark, he was able to maneuver around because he knew the layout of the home. On the front of his Glock was a single wolf silencer, perfectly made to suppress sound. Biggie tiptoed up the stairs and approached the first door. He quietly and slowly pushed it open. As he entered an older female was sleeping in the bed. Beside her lay her all white cat. His gun was aimed at her body as he approached the bed. Without further hesitation, he squeezed the trigger three times. His aim was precise as two shots landed inside of the woman's head and one shot tore the skull off of the white Persian cat.

As if he had just finished lunch and was ready to go, he turned around and walked out of the room. He then entered the next room down the hall. This time, the occupant was a young, sleeping teenage boy. Biggie aimed, fired, and two slugs made their permanent home into the young man's cranium.

Then Biggie entered the final bedroom of the house and was surprised to find a wide-awake young man lying on the bed watching TV. The young man jumped up from the bed, startled and scared for his life. He quickly put his hands up and said, "Please man don't hurt me!"

Seeing a midget, with a black ski mask, who was aiming his gun at this young man was not a typical scene, but nonetheless, the young man was filled with fear.

"What do you want," the man pleaded. "I just want you dead," Biggie said, as he squeezed the trigger precisely. Biggie played target practice with the man's head and chest.

After his victim's large body feel to the floor, Biggie pulled up his shirt and started to write on his chest with a black sharpie. *'I'm dead because my brother is a snitch,'* he etched onto his skin. Biggie went back into the other bedrooms and for the other young man, he wrote the same inscription, however for the mother he wrote- *Mother of a snitch: Fuck the FEDS* on her chest.

Then as quietly and low-key as Biggie had entered, he eased his way out of the house. He got back to his car and pulled off the down the street, blending into the night with other drivers.

No one hated snitches more than Biggie. It was because of a snitch his father was serving a life sentence at Lewisburg Federal Prison, in upstate Pennsylvania. Rats sickened him and for Biggie, anyone who associated themselves with a rat was just as guilty as the rat.

After King told Biggie about Rome's betrayal he made a personal decision to handle Rome's family. There was no way Biggie was going to allow any of Rome's family members to survive knowing that snitching ran through their blood. Biggie had seen too many good soldiers set up by rats, and it was a personal favorite of his to take them and their kin out. If he could kill every snitch in the world, he would, especially the one who was responsible for separating him from his father for a lifetime.

VI
CHELTEN AVENUE

Sitting outside of the Rose Peddles breakfast restaurant, King was reading the Daily Newspaper. When he came across the article about the triple homicide in North Philly all he could do was shake his head. His gut told him Biggie was behind it. He knew how much his friend hated snitches and whenever Biggie had important business to handle bodies always appeared days after.

Though King and Biggie were best friends, the two were complete opposites. Biggie had no patience, and if he was triggered, he made a move on you. King was calm; he liked to think things through before he had to act. He shared many of his cousin Face's take on things when it came to the game.

As King sat in his chair waiting for his breakfast order, he looked out the glass doors and noticed an attractive woman walking down the street. She was drop-dead gorgeous. Perfectly toned, light brown skin, 5'8, with a figure that was curvaceous in all the places that made the coolest men drool. This woman was giving Beyoncé a run for her money with no makeup on.

King was a young man, but he knew when he wanted something; and when he did, he made a move for it. He got up from the table and headed outside.

"Excuse me but I just wanted to tell you you're beautiful," he said to the young woman who turned around to see who was walking up behind her. As she stopped and turned to face King, he got a chance to look into her eyes.

They were as gray as the night's sky. She smiled, showing a perfect set of bright white teeth and King was pleased even more.

"So what's your name," he asked. King was a handsome young man with a substantial stature. His confidence was an immediate turn on, and the young woman softly replied, "Queen. My name is Queen." He chuckled at the irony of her name through him off. He asked, "Are you serious?" She continued to stare at him and smiled, and then said, "Yes. My father named me Queen twenty-four years ago, and it's been a pretty great name so far, so I'm sticking with it. That's my name."

"It's a beautiful name. They say every king needs a queen. My name is King so I guess I met mine," King said. "You're joking right," she asked as she laughed. "No more than you," he replied, as her smile lit up her entire face. "Queen, join me for breakfast so we can get to know each other better," he asked. "I wish I could, but I'm on my way to take care of some business. Maybe I can get a rain check," she said. "You shouldn't deny your King," he said jokingly. "But I understand."

They exchanged numbers, and each other's smile made it clear the two had instant chemistry with one another. King watched as Queen walked down the street and he couldn't help but think about her beauty. She had the perfect smile, and her face was flawless. He continued to stare at her until she had reached the corner.

As he sat down to eat his breakfast, he couldn't take his mind off of Queen. It wasn't as if he didn't have a score of other women to choose from but it was something special about this one that made him want to see her sooner than later.

Robert "Chino" Smith was King's first cousin and god-brother. Chino had gotten his nickname because of his slanted eyes. Most people thought he was mixed with Asian descent. Chino was light skinned, stocky, and well-liked by everyone in his Nicetown neighborhood. Just like King, they shared the same older cousin, Face, and both idolized him.

Inside his City Line Avenue apartment, Chino and his girlfriend, Khadijah were lying in bed. They had just finished fucking and were pretty worn out.

"So what's up with you today," she asked Chino. "I have some runs to make. What about you," he asked. "Well, I have a few places to go myself. I'm gonna go down South Philly later," she said. "You been going down there a lot lately. What's up with that," he asked, as he got up from the bed. "I told you, Bae, I'm spending some quality time with my mom and my sisters."

Chino sat down next to Kadijah and kissed her softly on the lips. For two years she had been the love of his life, and he couldn't see himself without his Kadijah. "Tell your mom I said hi and I'll see you later tonight. Love you," Chino said, as he got up and went to take a shower.

Once dressed, Khadijah walked Chino to the door and watched him pull off. Quickly she made her way back to the bedroom and pulled out her cellphone from her pocketbook.

"What's up am I seeing you today," a voice asked as she held her phone to her ear smiling. "Yes, I'm on my way to South Philly in a few," she said. "Okay, hurry up I miss you," the voice said. "I miss you more," Khadijah said, before ending the call.

Forty-five minutes later Kadijah walked out of the door and climbed into her brand new, all white Range Rover. It was a birthday gift that Chino has purchased for his love. He told her she was worth every penny. Her beauty and her sweet, soaking wet, tight pussy had him spoiling her every chance he got. Khadijah was a former model and Philadelphia Eagles cheerleader. Standing at 5'11 she always stood out and not for her height, but her incredible beauty.

As she headed towards South Philly, she turned on the radio. Lauren Hill flowed through her Bose speakers, and her mind started thinking about how great her day was about to be.

VII
60TH & GIRARD
WEST PHILLY

Vance Lewis stood two inches over six feet and had a very athletic body. His skin was as dark as coal, yet his eyes were bright hazel. He was forty-six years old but in amazing shape. When he was younger, he was a professional boxer with a good record and many knockouts.

When news spread that the former kingpin, Face, was retiring from the game, Vance began to build up his drug empire. He had a good portion of the city on lock; North, West, and parts of Southwest and South Philly. Vance was a violent man who demanded respect and ruled his crew with an iron fist. Together, he and his crew were responsible for over twenty murders, kidnappings and the torture of their victims. Vance had corrupt officers in his pockets and James McDuffie, a high-powered lawyer with a proven track record, was also on his payroll.

This vicious and violent man was the father of two incredibly beautiful daughters, whom he protected with all he had. When it came to his family, he was extremely private, and not even those closest to him knew much of anything about his home life.

Terry and Jerry Lucas, twin brothers who were impossible to tell apart, were close to Vance. The two light-brights stood at 5'8 and had the same robust build. They not only shared the same face and body structure, but their passion for killing was a mutual calling as well. Most likely they inherited this trait from their deceased uncle, Hood. He was a former drug boss who had been murdered by King's cousin, Face, several years earlier. The story of his death had always been a sore spot for the twins. Hearing that Face had their uncle's heart cut out made their hearts fill with hate. Their hatred for Face and King was evident; it was dark and very personal.

"King's responsible for this shit! That nigga is, I know it," Vance vented. The twins were speechless. They too had read the article about the triple homicide. "First they kill Rome, and now they kill his whole fuckin family! Who the fuck does King think he is," Vance continued. "Maybe they found out Rome was working for us," Terry said. "Maybe so but you don't kill the man's entire family. Is this young wannabe gangster trying to send a message," Vance questioned? "Maybe, it's payback for what we did to his friend Sammy a few months ago," Jerry added. "Fuck King, Fuck Biggie, and everyone else who riding with him! He's a young coward living off of his cousin's reputation! He's not Face, and he don't want war with me! I run Philly. I'm the boss now! Not Face, Not King!"

Terry and Jerry stood back and watched as their boss vented his anger. The murder of Rome was a hard pill for Vance to swallow. He was using Rome as a pawn to infiltrate King's drug organization. Rome was the key he needed to help destroy King's circle, and now he was dead along with his entire family.

For over a year, the two organizations had been at odds with each other as they set claims over the Philly drug market. Though King was only twenty years old, he had connections and made it difficult for Vance to run his empire the way he wanted too. As long as King stayed in the game his reach was limited, and Vance wanted it all. He was filled with greed and his ego, that was larger than life, would not allow a young punk to come in and run what he felt was his.

"I'm tired of playing this game with this little ass boy! I want his crew dead and of course, he dies with them! Better yet I want their families gone just like they took Rome's. Find me someone who can get me close to King, someone that knows his moves! We need to off him!"

"We on it boss! We got our people on the streets, and soon we gonna find those niggas and their peoples," Terry said. "Twenty-five stacks to anyone who gets me close to King and his crew," Vance said. "We got it," the Twins said in unison as they walked out the house.

Vance picked up his phone and called Johnny, one of the corrupt police officers that worked for him.

"Johnny what's up," Vance said. "I'll have some good news for you before the week is out," he said, bringing a smile to Vance's face. "That's what I want to hear," Vance said. "Don't worry man. We got Sammy, and we'll catch another one slipping as well," Johnny said, as his laughter echoed in the phone. "Yes, that was fun, and I need more enjoyment like that real soon. Very soon," Vance said. "You'll get it, boss. Just give me a few days," Johnny said before ending the call.

John Carter was a crooked police sergeant from the 18th district. For three years he had been working for Vance's drug organization. Johnny knew every move the officers, and the dealers made, and this gave Vance the opportunity to stay two steps ahead of his enemies. However, even with all of this crooked officer's connections, he was unable to get the drop on King. King had his network of protection, but Johnny was working hard to penetrate the wall. King appeared to be untouchable but Vance was no quitter, and he kept Johnny on the prowl. He knew this was like a game of chess and in the end, only one true king would be able to say checkmate.

VIII
33ʳᵈ & DIAMOND STREETS
THE PLAYGROUND

King was on the basketball court shooting jump shots. Every time he made a basket his bodyguard would retrieve the ball and pass it back to him. Before King became a drug dealer, he was one of the top basketball players in America. The 6'4, Kansas Jayhawks' high scoring, point guard, was a sure shot for the top 5 lottery pick in the NBA draft. Unfortunately, a significant knee injury during his junior year derailed his dream career in the NBA.

As King continued to shoot hoops, he watched as Biggie pulled up, parked, and then got out of his new Audi. King grabbed the ball and sat down on the bench, as Biggie walked up and sat down beside him. Nas was alert and stood guard as the two young men talked.

"What the hell were you thinking," King snapped. "Why would you kill Rome's family," he continued. Biggie looked directly into King's eyes and said, "Fuck all rats and their families! Too many good men are doing football numbers because of those rat ass niggas! They had to die." Face responded quickly, "You're not God! You ain't do nothing but kill three innocent people and bring unnecessary heat to us! The FEDS watching us, Vance is plotting against us, the Italians, Chinese, Columbian mobs all waiting for us to make a mistake! We ain't just some typical niggas with guns and money! We've got to be smarter Biggie!"

Biggie thought about what Face was saying and then he responded, "Fuck all those niggas, especially Vance. I won't ever forget what he did to Sammy! Never!" Face shook his head. Biggie's head was hard, and his rage needed taming. "We don't have to forget, but we gotta plan. It's a time and place for everything, and our moves need to be silent right now. There's too much heat on us."

Biggie was quiet as he thought about what Face was saying. He knew he was a hothead. At times, he let violence be his only answer, but he didn't want to bring and heat to what they were building. He was wrong, but there was nothing he could do that would bring Rome's family back. Moving forward, he promised King that he'd try to think before he acted.

"My bad. I'm working on this little temp and the next time I go on a rampage, I'll make sure just to get the targets I need to," Biggie swore. "I hope so because you killed eight people this month and you need to chill Lil Homie," King said. "Who the fuck you callin little," Biggie said, as they erupted into laughter. "Naw, but seriously I can't get over what they did to Sammy. They cut his fuckin head off! We buried our friend without a top, though. That shit wasn't cool."

King thought about the events that led up to Sammy's death. Sammy was the lieutenant in his organization, and they had been cool since second grade. A month and a half earlier he had been kidnapped. A passerby found his headless body on 19th & Hunting Park and everyone in the crew knew it was Sammy.

"As soon as Rome came around we lost three major shipments and Sammy. When you told me, he was a snitch I knew he was behind all of it. That nigga was working for Vance and trying to pick us off so Vance could take over. I ain't sorry for what I did. They deserved it, but I promise you I'll think before I make another move like that. I'll get you to sign my permission slip first," Biggie said, causing the young men to laugh.

"Yeah, we gotta be smarter, though. We got eyes on us, and everyone wants the crown. I know you an aggressive little nigga, but you gotta calm your ass down. We got work to move and money to make. How's the shipments moving," King ask in a serious tone? "Moving good. We will have the money back tonight, and these new moves have made us living legends. Face set us up right. A couple million is expected back tonight."

After they had shaken hands, King watched Biggie get back in his car and drive off. The plan was to meet back up later in the evening with the entire crew. They were making more money than anyone of them could have imagined, but King needed to discuss his next moves and his vision with each of them.

As he went back to shooting his precise jump shot, his personal cellphone started to ring. The smile that quickly appeared on his face made it clear he was pleased with the caller.

"Hello Queen," he said. "Hi King, what's up with you," she asked. "Nothing, shooting hoops and thinking about you," he said, as he made another perfect shot. "Oh really," she smiled. "Yes really, when can we link up," King asked. "I'm free later tonight. I'll text you when I'm ready," she said, before hanging up the phone.

IX
BALA CYNWYD, PA

Vance stood in his doorway and watched as the gray BMW parked. A tall, beautiful black woman got out of the car and walked towards him. They greeted by kissing each other's lips before he asked the woman, "How was your day at the office today?" She smiled and said, "Work is work. Clients never stop coming and going. That's my job."

He led her into the house, caressing her shoulders until they got into the living room. "You're one of the best at what you do," he said unsnapping her bra. After Vance had undressed the slim, beautiful woman, he said, "Are you ready for your bad boy?" Seductively she replied, "I'm always ready for you Daddy."

Vance stood behind the woman and bent her over the custom-made marble table. He then spread her legs apart and gripped her hips. Then Vance got down on his knees and started to eat her warm, dripping, appetizing pussy from behind.

"Don't move baby you're in my courtroom now, and I'm your Judge," he demanded. Her legs trembled, and she did her best to stay still; even though each time he thrust his tongue deep into her pussy she couldn't help but quiver. Her pussy vibrated as his tongue took control. She could barely handle his tongue as her orgasm came to a head. Her echoing moans filled the house. Vance was eager, and he took no time inserting his massive, solid, hard dick deep inside of her. She braced herself as he fucked her pussy intensely and demanded she answer his questions.

"Who do you belong to," he asked, fucking her harder each time he finished his sentences. "You daddy! I belong to you," she yelled, enjoying each moment of this fuck session. "Whose pussy is it," he asked. "Yours, Yours, Yours," she shouted as her pussy juices squirted all over his body.

For three years Vance and his female lover had been having a secret relationship. They had met at one of the murder trials he was acquitted on, and it was best they kept their association private. If anyone found out about them, there would be chaos and her career would be in jeopardy.

BAY OF KOTOR, MONTENEGRO

Named one of the most exotic vacation destinations in the world, The Boka, as it is known, is surrounded by emerald waters and picturesque mountains.

"You enjoying your trip around the world so far," Quincy asked Face. "Yeah, my family needed this vacation. "What's up in Philly," he asked. "King is handling his business, and he knows what he has to do if he wants to stay on top," Quincy replied. "Continue to keep me posted. That's my Lil cousin, and I want him to be safe in those streets. Philly can be the biggest gift and curse for a hustler," Face said. "Don't I know it, but I got my eyes on King. You still want me to keep my distance because you know I can play him close," Quincy asked. "Yeah, he's gotta start being on point. He can't have his hand held forever. I have to let him learn from his mistakes," Face said. "Okay. I'll keep my ears to the streets and let you know if anything major comes up."

LATER THAT EVENING

The Twins sat inside of a dark green Cadillac Escalade. Beside each was a loaded A-K47. Every night they would drive around the city and look for targets. Any rival drug dealers were fair game, and if they came in contact, kidnapping, torture, and a killing was surely on the agenda. In just under two years the Twins had murdered over thirty men, women, and children. And thanks to their high-powered lawyer anything that came their way was discarded in court due to lack of evidence and witnesses.

73rd & OGANTZ AVENUE

King looked on as his crew sat around a large table counting endless stacks of money. This was a part of their routine. They had the best product, best prices, and being connected to the best; King brought in the most money.

While everyone was counting and packing money inside of large duffle bags, Biggie stood by the window on a footstool holding a loaded .357 magnum. Even though King had hired hands outside the front, back, and side of their location, Biggie took no chances when it came to their safety. If anyone unauthorized would have approached the house or breached the door, he was ready.

When the money was packaged, and the count was recorded, the bags were loaded in the trunks of two police cruisers and headed off to a secret location in the Northeast. King also had a connection with crooked cops and for twenty thousand dollars a month, these two officers were always willing to do whatever King and his crew needed.

Once the cash was delivered, King headed to a secret location to meet with the Columbians. He needed to make arrangements for them to pick up a new shipment of pure heroin and cocaine. He became very cautious about the moves he made and how he made them. Now King always had a game plan, and if anything didn't feel right, he was determined to trust his gut and get ghost. There were only three people he could trust with his life, Biggie, Chino, and Face. So now everything was about being cautious since he had moved up the food chain and too many people wanted his spot.

When he was done with his business for the day, King made his way to his next destination. He had something personal lined up that he was anticipating, a date with the beautiful Queen.

X

"Bitch shut the fuck up," Terry said, as he slapped the frightened woman senselessly. Terry and Jerry had just kidnapped a rival drug dealer's wife. They caught her alone closing up her hair salon on South Street.

Twenty minutes after the abduction she was inside of a basement, blindfolded, and handcuffed. She had never been more frightened in all of her life. Terry snatched off her blindfold while Jerry took the handcuffs off of her. Then Jerry passed the frantic woman her cell phone.

"Call that nigga now bitch," Terry yelled. The woman did as she was ordered. "Baby where are you," her husband said. Before she had a chance to reply she screamed, "Plex they got me!" "Who got you," he asked becoming anxious. Terry snatched the phone out of her hand.

"The Twins muthafucka," he said. "Yo, what do you want man! Just tell me and I'll get it but please don't hurt my wife," Plex pleaded. "You should've thought about that when I gave you the warning months ago! We told you to come work on this side or retire, but your fuckin hearing was off," Terry snapped. "I will retire! I don't need this shit this bad," Plex pleaded. "Just don't hurt my wife!"

Jerry listened on speaker phone as Plex begged for his wife's life to be spared. Terry placed a .40 cal into the woman's mouth, and she began to scream out as much as she could. "Too late," Jerry said, as Terry pulled the trigger and blew a hole through the back of the woman's head.

Plex cried out for answers, but the Twins ended the call. They ignored the persistent ringing phone as they began wrapping the corpse inside of a large area rug. The two picked up the rug and carried it out to their car. Once the body was placed inside of their trunk, they drove to West Philly to one of their favorite dumping spots.

Less than an hour later the Twins were sitting at a table inside of Friday's restaurant on City Line Avenue. They had ordered drinks and were eating crispy fried Buffalo wings. The game was on, and the Philadelphia 76ers were getting blown out by Miami, but the men still celebrated the day's events. They were pleased with their actions and looked forward to the next day's adventures.

325 CHESTNUT STREET

Buddakan restaurant was spacious and opulent, centered around a ten-and-a-half foot gold gilded Buddha. The upscale, five-star eatery was visited by many for not only their décor but their delicious, well-seasoned, and tasty menu.

Near the back of the restaurant, King and Queen sat at a private table. King couldn't help but stare at the incredible beauty who sat directly across from him. Queen observed her environment and wasn't impressed with the restaurant, or the type of people inside of it.

"Do you really like this spot," she asked. "Yes, the food is really good here, and the decor is pretty dope, "King said. Queen smiled softly and sat deep in her chair. "What, you don't like it, "King asked. "The restaurant is alright but the vibe from the people, not so much. Everyone in here is so stiff and fake acting. Spending all this money on something we can get from the corner Chinese store," she said.

King reached over and took Queen's hands into his and began to rub them gently. "Listen we can go wherever you want. I want you to be comfortable," he said. "Can we leave now," she asked. "Sure," he said, standing up and walking towards her to pull her chair out.

As they walked out of the door, Queen was impressed. She loved when a man put her wants at the forefront, and he had made a great impression on her. King was handsome, kind, educated and she knew by the way he dressed and spent money, he wasn't hurting for any. If he continued giving into her needs and wants she could see herself spending a lot of quality time with him.

While they walked to the car, he asked, "So where do you want to go?" "If you're not too boogie I'd like to go to the Crab House on Germantown Avenue." King knew the exact location of the Crab House. Often it was filled with low levels dealers, gangsters, hood chicks, pimps, homeless folks, and your average Joes. It wasn't a place that he'd pick, but they certainly had a reputation for having excellent seafood, and the drinks were always made to get you feeling nice.

On their way to the Crab House, King and Queen had a lengthy conversation, and they learned more about one another. King learned that Queen had another side to her. The beautiful Queen could be a beast when she wanted or needed to be. She had a short fuse and her tolerance for petty people, and the games they played were never taken lightly. Also, she wasn't afraid to speak her mind, and he liked that. He wasn't attracted to Yes women.

Sitting in the Crab House, both noticed they were being watched by several sets of eyes. It seemed like everyone was whispering about the couple but neither took it severe enough to leave. King knew he was well-known in the city and to see a Boss sitting with a beautiful woman was surely enough to have eyes on them and lips whispering.

"I'll be right back handsome," Queen said, as she stood up to go to the ladies room. As soon as she was out of sight a dark skinned beauty approached King at their table.

"Hey cutie, my name is Joy. I noticed your tall sexy ass when you walked in. Take my number and call me when you get free. Tonight if you want to," she said smiling as she passed him her number. Before she could walk away, Queen was standing right behind her.

"Dirty bitch are you serious right now," Queen said, as anger filled her face. Everyone in the club focused in on them to see what was going on. "I should beat the shit out of your black, thirsty, desperate ass right now! You disrespectful ass ho!"

Queen swiftly pulled and wrapped Joy's untamed weave around her left hand. In her right hand, she had a blade placed at Joy's face.

"If it wasn't so many people in here I wouldn't think twice," she said, as she unloosened her grip and pushed Joy down to the floor. The woman was embarrassed and quickly got her purse and rushed out of the bar.

King was speechless; his Queen had turned into Biggie right before his eyes. Where did her rage come from, he thought? It was unexpected, but surprisingly he liked it.

"Babe can we get out of here before I kill one of these thirsty lowlife bitches," she said, giving him a smile. "Sure, where do you want to go," King said settling the bill. "Anywhere as long as it's not in Germantown," Queen replied. "Anywhere," King said, with a devilish grin as the two got into his Mercedes and sped down Chelten Avenue.

The sounds of intense sexual randevú filled the air inside of the luxurious hotel suite. Inside, Biggie had two beautiful women laid across the bed in their birthday suits. Condoms, an ounce of Exotic, a small package of powder cocaine, Peach Cîroc, a large bottle of Hennessy, and some cash lay on the table next to the bed.

The three had been at their lustful ménage for a few hours. Silver and Diamond were two strippers who worked at Onyx. As Silver fucked Diamond with her tongue, Biggie was behind Silver thrusting himself inside of her. Although Biggie was short, his dick was bigger than most men double his size. He had a very thick sausage that filled up any hole. Women never doubted Biggie's sexual abilities after sleeping with him.

Biggie was known in the club as a big spender and a man who loved to party. The ladies felt lucky if they caught his eye and got to spend some time with him outside of the club. Not only would their pockets be filled up but their pussies would also be pleased with the amount of dick he stuffed inside of them.

Biggie was like a shorter, black version of Hugh Heffner because he never left with just one girl. They swarmed to him like bees to honey, and he always had enough cash and dick for whoever came with him.

Tonight Silver and Diamond were the chosen ones and their night was filled with sex, drugs, and alcohol. Each received two-thousand dollars for being a part of his sex games.

Biggie pulled his dick out of Silver and placed it inside of Diamond's mouth. She was very talented, and as he began to cum in her mouth, Biggie started to pound on his chest. He grabbed her long blonde weave as the final drops of his cum dripped in her mouth and asked, "What's my name?" Seductively and with cum dripping out of her mouth she said, "Biggie Daddy."

But the fun was now over. Biggie didn't trust them no matter how good they sucked a dick or how tight and wet their pussies were. He always kept his gun close by, and once he was done an Uber was called to escort them to their next destination.

MANAYUNK

Zeta and her sexy girlfriend, Tasty, were cuddled up on the sofa as Zack sat on the floor hypnotized watching his favorite cartoons.

"Babe I can't do it anymore. I'm tired of stripping, and I'm done with the club life. Once I stack some more bread I'm opening up a hair salon downtown," Tasty said. Zeta knew Tasty was serious about leaving the club, but she needed her in position for just a bit more. She also needed to test her loyalty to see if she was the woman she could splurge on completely. Zeta had enough money to open up a salon for Tasty, but right now she needed her to keep put.

"Give me a few months and then you can quit. I promise you I'll take care of you. You know how many people come through those doors that we need to see. So do this for me, okay," Zeta asked. "Okay, just a few more months and then I'm done. I'll keep my eyes open and tell you and King anything y'all need to know, but when my times up I'm out of there."

Zeta pulled her arms tighter around her girlfriend and gave her a quick kiss for comfort and reassurance.

CAMDEN, NEW JERSEY

Inside the tinted black van, a tall Latin man named Carlos was moving 150 kilos of pure Columbian cocaine. Carlos was a driver and drug distributor for one of the most violent cartels in the Tri-State. He was driving to Philly to drop off his delivery. Unbeknownst to Carlos he was being watched the entire time. As soon as the van crossed the Ben Franklin Bridge into Philadelphia, he was ambushed as a swarm of vehicles surrounded him. Two masked men ran up on Carlos with guns aimed at his head. Terror filled his face as the men yelled, "Don't move muthafucka!" Carols didn't move. He was so scared that his body had already frozen before the men told him to.

When the contents of Carlos' vehicle were cleared and placed in a van, the men quickly sped off in different directions. Now he was free to move but didn't want to. It dawned on him he'd have to answer for his loss. Maybe a bullet in the head might have been better than what was now awaiting him.

...

"I just text Vance and let him know everything went well," one of the men said. "Okay, let's drop this shit off to the sergeant," another one of the men said. "But yo, this shit is crazy. We robbed one drug dealer just to take it all to a crooked cop, who then takes it to another drug dealer. This is an ugly game," the man said.

XII
NORTHERN LIBERTIES

Some of Philadelphia's ghettos and impoverished areas had significant revamping done on them. So much so it was hard to tell these vacant, filthy, dilapidated zones even existed. Northern Liberties was once one of these areas but with a new name it was now known as a city's hotspot; attracting affluent investors, entrepreneurs, and new and old money back to the neighborhood.

Inside of King's newly renovated luxurious condo, Queen lay nestled in his arms on his plush, imported European sofa. The sixty inch, smart television hung on the wall as they watched the latest episode of Empire. During a commercial break, Queen took that moment to suck on King's bottom lip.

"I just wanted to taste it," she said. "It's just as sweet as I thought it would be." He smiled but didn't speak. He wanted her bad, and although he hated to admit it, he was a little nervous. Queen could be intimidating.

Her eyes glanced down to see what had risen inside of King's pants, and she was very pleased to see his imprint. Queen placed her hands on his new growth and began to stroke his dick, causing it to rise more. Suddenly she stopped and softly said, "I'll be back. I have to go to the bathroom."

King watched as she walked away. Each moment she was gone he wondered what he should do when she returned. When she returned, she was now nude, and all he could do was stare at her flawless body. Her body was like one of a sex goddess and she smelled tasty.

"Don't say a word," Queen demanded. King did as he told and sat as Queen took his hands and placed them behind his back. "Don't touch me and don't talk to me or I'm going to stop. Can you do that?" King nodded his head in agreement, playing along with her. Queen knelt down and pulled down King's jeans and gray Polo briefs until they hung around his ankles. She looked at his lengthy, thick dick. Then she opened her mouth, gliding his big dick down her warm, saliva coated throat.

"Dammmnnnnn," he said, impressed with her deep-throat skills. "It tastes so goooood," Queen said, as she pulled his long dick from her throat. "Wait one minute," she said, before getting up and walking towards the kitchen. King was left craving her warm mouth.

When she returned, she held a small jar of honey in her hand. King watched as Queen got back down on her knees. She placed an ample amount of honey on his dick and started giving him one of the stickiest, sloppiest, dick sucks he had ever had! His mind was blown. King was trembling. His legs were turning into limp noodles as she gulped down his dick and slurped up the honeysuckle she had spread all over him. Queen was no amateur, and she had his full attention.

"I want you," he said, bringing his hands from behind his back and placing them on her head. Queen looked up at him and their eyes locked. She gave one strong, final slurp and then she stood up.

"What's wrong," he asked, noticing her mood had changed instantly. "I told you not to talk or touch me, right," she said, wiping her mouth. "The dick suck was free, but this pussy has to be earned."

SOUTH PHILLY
INSIDE A ROW HOUSE ON 17ᵀᴴ STREET

King, Chino, Zark and Biggie sat at a table inside one of their stash houses talking.

"So what's up with this new chick Queen," Chino asked. "I like her. Yeah, she's cool," King said, trying to be cool but his healthy smile gave him away. "Damn she got you pussy-whipped already homey," Biggie said, causing them to erupt into laughter. "Whipped, naw, we ain't go there yet. She's a good girl. I just dig her style, and she's real. I like her, though," King said. "Well, I can tell your times being occupied by somebody and I don't recall the king ever taking this long to get some pussy from a chick. What you fell off," Zark said. King just smiled.

Chino looked at King and said, "I'm your god brother, and I've been around your whole life, and I ain't never seen you turned out like this before. She got you open. You ain't even get like this over Keisha Jackson, and she had your ass turned out in high school. You remember Keisha, right," Chino said laughingly. "Damn, she got you so sprung you forgot about Keisha. Let me get some," he continued, making everyone laugh even more. "Man I remember Keisha, but this girl's something different. I can't explain it, and Y'all gonna stop clowning me. I like the girl, that's it," King said, as he watched Zark dump a pile of cash on the table from the large green duffle bag that was on the floor.

"We have a few shipments coming in over the next few weeks," King said, quickly changing the mood of the room from jokes to straight business. "Ant Love is trying to get a hundred bricks this time," he continued. "Oh, he stepping his game up, huh," Biggie said, as he put a stack of bills through the money counting machine. "I don't trust that dude for some reason. I never liked him," Chino said thoughtfully. "Yo, Ant been riding with us for over three years now," Biggie said. "I know that, but I just don't like the vibe I'm feeling from him sometimes," Chino said. "Chill out Chino and stop being paranoid. We got more product and a lot more money coming our way now so we all a little skeptical, but ain't no need to go starting shit over fabricated vibes," Zark said.

King sat back listening as the three men continued to talk and count money. Chino was King's lieutenant, and they had known each other since they were kids. Most times Chino had been on point when it came to his intuition, and other times it was totally off. King didn't want to discredit his vibe, especially now that they had more to lose- but way more to gain if they used their head wisely in the business. He couldn't risk being paranoid, and he didn't want to live scared; just wiser.

After they counted up a little over a half a million dollars and loaded it into the back of King's Mercedes, King looked at Chino and said, "Stop stressing over nothing. We good God-brother." Chino smiled and said, "I know, right. It's just crazy because this shit is all too real. We up, like up for real, and I want us to stay up for good. I've had shit on my mind, and I had a fucked up dream last night, but I gotta chill."

King didn't like the mention of dreams. He didn't think they were coincidental. However, with Chino, he could be so extra so you just never knew with him.

"What was your dream about," King asked. Chino replied, "Death." "Whose death," King asked. "I couldn't see the face. I only saw a body on the ground in a pool of blood." "Ain't that the same dream you had a few months ago," King asked, as he chuckled. "I'm serious King! This shit felt real," Chino snapped.

King saw the seriousness in Chino's eyes and said, Man, we good! Don't worry. I promised Aunt Pattie I'd take care of you, and that's what I'm doing. So chill out Chino."

Chino shook his head in agreement and then said, "Yeah, I know right. I just don't want shit to happen to us. We always watching our backs from the FEDS, these dealers, and all these fuckin haters and rats!" "Chino we too thick to start bitchin now! Face made his decision, and I'm good with it. I hold the torch and Y'all my crew! Ain't no quit in me and we good," he said firmly.

Chino wasn't trying to convince his god brother to leave the game, but just to be cautious. They had been so close to being shut down by Rome, and Sammy having his head cut off because they caught him off-guard made Chino leery.

"King you're not Face. He was a legend in this game and dudes feared him so much they didn't want to be on the same block as him. We don't have that luxury yet. We gotta watch our backs because he won't be there all the time," Chino shouted. "I'm not Face! And I'm not trying to be, but I learned a lot from him. If I couldn't handle what's ours, then you wouldn't be here right now. I'm here because I'm ready for this, so you're here because you're ready! Don't second guess me because I don't want to second guess you! Just play your part and I got us," King said, sending a clear message to his god brother and the rest of his crew.

MOUNT AIRY

Inside of a large home, Vance stood as he talked on his cellphone.

"Are you sure man," he said into his phone. "I'm positive. It's all set up," said the voice on the other end. "Okay then and if you're right about this, I'll make sure you're well taken care of. Just make sure you get me all the details," Vance said. "I sure will. No worries," the man said before ending the call.

"What's the deal Bossman," Terry asked. "I got some real good news fellas," Vance said grinning. "What is it," Jerry curiously asked. Vance looked at the Twins and said, "I got King's bitch ass! My peoples just put me down!"

The Twins sat down in shock as Vance begin to tell them everything he had learned.

THREE DAYS LATER
IN THE EARLY MORNING

Plex pulled up and parked his car in the back of the Philadelphia Zoo. He was accompanied by one of his closest friends. The area had been taped off with yellow police tape. A crowd of onlookers stood behind the tape taking pictures and capturing video on the cell phones. They were also speculating as to what had happened. Yellow police tape often was synonymous with a homicide in the city of Philadelphia; whose nickname was now Killadelphia due to the rising homicide rate.

Two joggers had discovered a woman's corpse and immediately they notified police. Once the police arrived, they searched her body for identification and to see if she had anything on her they could use to locate any relatives or friends. Through a police search in their headquarters, they learned she was married and were able to contact the deceased's husband.

When Plex exited the car, he was filled with an eerie feeling. He knew he wasn't summoned here because there was going to be good news. As he approached the detective, the unnerving feeling returned and weighed on him like a ton of sorrows.

Nervously, the detective escorted him to the crime scene and pulled back the sheet, exposing the body. His wife of four years, the woman he had loved and adored, lay lifeless on the cold concrete. The scene was horrific and brutal for any eyes, but to see his wife's face blown away was too much for any husband to view. His tears soared and his legs buckled as his friend tried to keep him upright.

The detective asked him to come down to the district for questioning, but Plex refused. He was filled with rage, and there was no confusion as to who was responsible. He promised himself he wouldn't rest until he settled the score with those responsible for his wife's grisly death.

Vance, the Twins, and anyone else who had something to do with him losing the love of his life was now wearing a target on their backs. He wanted blood, and the taste of hate would never leave his mouth until his enemies blood ran from their bodies!

XIII
TWO MONTHS LATER

Within eight weeks, King and Queen had grown closer, and it wasn't because of any bedroom escapades. They still hadn't had sex and even though Queen had given King more of her energy draining, mind-blowing dick sucks, the two were connecting on other levels.

The energy they shared was priceless, and though they talked a lot about themselves, their likes, dislikes, and goals; neither would exchange information about their family. King certainly didn't feel the need to talk about what he did for a living, even if Queen had assumptions. He had no desire to tell her he was one of the biggest drug dealers on the East coast, nor did King want her to know he was passed the reigns from his well-known, legendary, kingpin cousins, Face.

King made the challenging decision to lie to her. He told her he had his knees and legs insured for a multi-million dollar policy when he played college ball. That his uncle had given him the idea to do so when he saw a college ball player's leg bone rip through his skin on a hard fall. And since he had injured himself he was glad to have listened to his uncle. He didn't question whether she believed him because she didn't question him, and that was because she held her own secrets in her closet.

Queen sat down on the edge of her bed admiring King's naked tall, dark athletic physique.

"You're so damn sexy," she said as she started kissing his chest. "So when are you going to let me," Queen placed her finger over kings mouth, hushing his words. "Soon handsome, very soon. Have a little patience. I want to know you're worthy. I told you before I don't share my man or my dick. So I have to be sure you want me exclusively before we go to the next level," she said seductively.

"You are the only one I want. I told you I cut ties with whoever I was talking to because it was never anything serious. I want you," King said, feeling sexually frustrated but trying to be patient. "You told me that you had a friend for a few years, and I never pushed the issue with you. Maybe I shouldn't let you put my dick up in your mouth until I know you're done with whoever you were messing with," King said, showing some of his frustration.

Queen didn't allow his hissy-fit to change her mind. She was unbending, and she knew specifically what she was doing and how she was going to do it.

Queen laid King down on his back and climbed on top of him, with her ass facing his mouth and her face towards his feet. She placed her soaking wet pussy over top of his mouth and let her nectar drip onto his lips. As he opened his mouth, she lowered her kitty perfectly for him to get a full taste of her pussy. As soon as his mouth made contact she deep-throated his dick; causing him to fall deeper into the bed. He tried to stay in control and give her pussy the right attention, but each time his dick met her tonsils he felt like exploding.

When he could no longer fight his urge to ejaculate he burst, sending his warm sperm deep inside of her mouth. Simultaneously she squirted into his mouth and soaked his face and the bed. Both collapsed onto each other, feeling as if they had just fucked for hours.

XIV
42nd & MANTUA AVENUE
WEST PHILLY

After the kidnapping and murdering of his wife, Plex hadn't been the same. His hatred for Vance and the Twins escalated each moment he realized they had warm blood running through their bodies. He wanted revenge, and no moral compass could give him a change of heart.

Day and night he and one of his closest hit men, scoured the streets looking for Vance, the Twins, and members of their crew. He had made a promise and with his loaded AK-47 and an MAC-10, he would get the blood he required.

Plex was desperate for revenge. He hired a private investigator to find him any information that would lead him to his enemies. However, finding info on Vance and the Twins was harder than he thought. Many people were tightlipped, and details were few because they often traveled in secret.

"Let's go back to North," Plex told his driver. He made a quick U-turn and drove down Girard Avenue. Plex looked out of the windows as they drove past the Philadelphia Zoo. He had a stoic look on his face, and his mind was deeply lost in his thoughts. Someone had to die. Someone would die. Vance and the Twins were on borrowed time.

BROAD & FAIRMOUNT
EARLY THE NEXT MORNING

Biggie tailed behind one of the transport vans as he listened to the police scanner. Inside of the truck were 100 kilos of cocaine, hidden inside of one hundred X-Box consoles. It was a weekly trip that Biggie oversaw, along with several other shipments that made their way through the city of Philadelphia.

Chino drove as Zark played passenger and lookout. Zeta rode ahead of the detail on a blue and black Suzuki GSX-R600 motorcycle. King didn't want to take any chances. He took as many precautions as he could to secure his transports reached their final destinations safely.

When the van stopped at a red light on 9th & Fairmount Streets, two cars quickly sped up from behind and pulled in front of the truck. Within seconds five men had jumped out of those vehicles, rushed the van and opened fire; using their semi-automatic weapons. Spectators begin to scream and run for cover as this scene from out of a movie played out in the streets in broad daylight.

Biggie jumped into gear as he rushed from his car and began firing his AK-47. He was able to quickly take out one of the masked men while the others did their best to dodge his lethal assault. Zeta drove her motorcycle on the payment as she rushed towards the van. She pulled her gun and shot one of the mask men who was trying to get back into his car. It was an instant kill shot. One of the other men made it to the van. He threw Chino from the driver's seat and onto the ground, as Zark leaped out, barely dodging a bullet meant for his head. The other two masked men rushed back into their car and sped off.

During the assault, Chino and Zark didn't have a chance to reach for their weapons because they were caught completely off guard. Chino had taken several fatal headshots, and Zark was fighting for his life. He was shot but didn't know exactly where. There was blood everywhere, and he was in intense pain. Biggie assisted the severely injured Zark.

As the masked man drove the van away, Zeta followed on her motorcycle and gave chase to the bullet-riddled van. She was firing off what bullets she had left until she was empty. She continued to trail him until he went down a one-way street and she noticed a cop car in the adjacent area. She quickly headed towards a secluded alleyway and parked her bike. She removed her jacket, pulled her hair out of her ponytail and tried to blend into society as she looked for another getaway.

Back at the scene, Biggie could hear the sirens approaching as he helped Zark up and into his car. He looked over at Chino, and there was nothing he could do for him. A portion of his brain was blown out of his head; he was dead. His anger at the site of his friend sent him over to one of the already dead masked men. He sent more of his bullets into the head of the man, ultimately rendering him faceless as Zark softly and painfully cried out, "Let's go." Biggie rushed back to the car and sped off.

Zeta found a cab. She was speechless when he asked, "Where to?" The early morning battle had taken the life of one of their beloved crew members, and one hundred kilos of pure cocaine was unaccounted for.

XV
TWENTY MINUTES LATER

The bullet-ridden van pulled up and parked in the back of a garage on Ridge Avenue. Wounded and limping, Terry got out of the van holding onto his arm. He was shot in both his leg and arm, but the damage wasn't severe. He was aided by Toney, who was waiting for the men to return.

A few moments later the car pulled up, which had more holes in it than the van and no windows at all. Terry pulled off his mask. He watched as one man got out the car and pulled his mask off. It was Carvin. He said, "Ab's dead. His passenger had sustained several gunshot wounds and bled to death.

"Where's my brother," Terry cried out. Carvin hung his head low. They had lost three men and Jerry was one of them. He didn't make it back from the scene and thanks to Biggie he no longer had a face.

Jerry has lost his twin brother. He sobbed knowing the other half of him was gone forever. Jerry felt empty and dead. It was like he had a body but it had been emptied out. His soul has ceased to exist. He would have accepted the loss of the other men; he'd preferred that, but not his brother. He was not supposed to lose his right hand. He was in inconsolable pain.

Vance walked into the garage fuming. "What the fuck went wrong! No one was supposed to get killed! This shit was meant to be a sweet pick," he yelled. "That fuckin midget jumped out with, and AK and then this bitch drove up on a bike blasting," Carvin said. "I promise I'm killing that bitch and that little nigga! They killed my fuckin brother Vance," Terry exploded.

Vance walked over and placed his hand on Terry's shoulder. "I give you my word you will get to pay them back," he promised. "Carvin, Toney, start taking that work out. It's inside of those X-Boxes."

Just like Vance said, they had inherited 100 kilos of cocaine hidden inside the empty game consoles.

"I need to clear my head," Terry said. "I'm going to kill King, "Terry repeated. He rushed out of the garage bleeding and in need of medical care.

Vance watched as his top lieutenant walked away with his heart heavy and his head hung. He could only imagine the pain Terry was enduring; however he had to put his focus on the prize he had just won.

Once all kilos were placed inside of the trunk of his car, Vance hurried inside of his vehicle and drove off. He was pleased to have lightened King's load, and now he knew Terry would be more inclined to bring him his enemies' head. Things were exactly how Vance wanted and needed them to be.

On the top floor of a three-story apartment building, King angrily paced the floor. His entire crew watched in silence as King tearfully vented his anger. His godbrother was brutally slain and his good friend, Zark was in Hahnemann Hospital in critical condition.

In less than a year he had lost two influential members in his drug origination. The death of each had taken a toll on him.

"What went wrong," he yelled out. "How the hell did they know our exact location?" No one said a word. They had never seen King this angry before. They were used to his calm demeanor but today he was anything but himself.

"They killed my fuckin god-brother," he cried out. "They killed Chino," he screamed.

No one knew what to say, and they kept silent as King walked to the window and stared out at the sky. They were feeling the pain of their anguish.

"They got us for a hundred kilos and my brother is dead! Somebody has got to pay for this Biggie and we gettin our shit back," King burst out as he stormed out and made his way to his car.

As he drove to his apartment, the tears didn't miss a beat as they poured from his eyes. Hearing his cell phone beep, he looked at the text message.

I'm sorry about your loss today baby. It's all over the news. I liked Chino; he was a real dude. Just know he's' in a better

place and if you need me, call me. If you don't feel like talking, you can text me too. I'm here for you.
Love

Your Queen

King pulled his car over and parked. He didn't want to be alone, and he needed the comfort of someone he could trust.

I need you, Queen. Meet me at my apartment as soon as you can.

King

As he started to drive home, his mind replayed images of Chino's face. His eyes carried the picture in each tear he shed. He was overwhelmed and tonight was going to be a long one. He thought about Chino's dream and how he had brushed it off. He had told Chino there was nothing to worry about. King now wished he had taken Chino's vision serious, because what he had called paranoia was now a living nightmare. A nightmare that he'd have to relive for the rest of his life.

XVII
9:05 P.M.
WEST PHILLY

A black Ford Taurus pulled up and parked across the street from a row home on 38th and Reno Streets. Terry and Carvin sat inside their car watching as a constant swarm of traffic went in-and-out of the door. This house was a known drug spot, generating over ten-thousand dollars a day in profits. It was run by Trouble, one of King's loyal street soldiers.

Terry sat stone-faced with murder inscribed in his eyes. The death of his brother continued to play in his mind, and he wanted to kill someone to help him deal with his pain. At this point, it didn't matter who it was, but it was certainly going to be someone inside of King's organization. Terry was out for revenge.

As soon as the crowd of addicts had slowed up, Terry reacted. Underneath his seat were two live hand grenades. At this moment, it was his weapon of choice and defense he had used many times before. Carvin sat behind the wheel and watched as Terry opened the door and got out of the car. Calmly, Terry walked over to the house.

"Is Trouble inside," Terry asked, with his hands inside of his pockets, clutching the two hand grenades. "Yeah, what do you want he's a little busy right now," the man said. Terry took one of the grenades from out of his pocket, walked away from the man and popped the pin.

"I want his life," Terry said, before throwing the grenade at the stunned man.

Boooom!!! The explosion damaged the front of the house. Through the fire and debris, Terry could hear the house full of people crying out in agony. They had no clue as to what had just hit them, and many were now in need of serious medical care.

Terry didn't hesitate as he threw the other grenade inside the house. Boooom!!! The second explosion went off. Calmly the cold hearted killer turned and walked back over to the car.

The screams of burn victims could be heard clearly in the night air. Those who could walk began to rush from the house, dazed, confused, and scorched. Smoke was everywhere, and the fire started to engulf other houses. The sounds of approaching cop cars and paramedics were now in the mix as they got closer to the scene.

"I promise you, brother, I'm going to kill all of them," Terry said, as Carvin drove them away from the blood-filled, fire burning, and smoke-filled scene.

XVIII
9:15 P.M.
18TH & TASKER STREETS
SOUTH PHILLY

For the past two hours, Zeta and Biggie had been watching a home very carefully. They were parked in a van a half block away, watching everything with a high scope pair of binoculars.

"Did you see what I saw," Zeta asked Biggie? "Yeah, I saw that no good bitch! Now I understand everything," he said, shaking his head in disgust. "I never trusted that whore," he vented.

Biggie called King on his untraceable cell phone and reported to his boss what Zeta and he had observed. King couldn't believe it, and moments later, King and his bodyguard Nas pulled up in a gray Honda Accord.

Once they were assembled, they exited their cars. Each strapped with loaded pistols and wearing bulletproof vests. As they walked over to the house, Biggie began to play around with the doorknob. A few seconds later the doorknob turned, and Biggie slowly pushed the door open. Biggie walked inside, and King and Zeta followed behind closely.

From their surveillance, they knew only two people were inside the house. With their guns clutched in their hands, they tiptoed up the stairs. As they got closer to the top of the stairs, they could hear the sounds of passionate moans and intense groans coming from the room.

They approached the front bedroom and heard a male ask, "Whose pussy is this bitch!" A female voice yelled out, "It's yours, Daddy! All yours!"

Without further delay Biggie, Zeta and King all burst through the door with their guns pointed at the two naked lovers. They were shocked and afraid.

"Oh my God," Khadijah shouted, as she quickly grabbed the sheet to cover her exposed body. "Aww, shit," Ant Love yelled. "Please man just let me explain," he said, placing his hands up in the air.

King walked over to Ant Love and put his 9mm to his forehead. "Yall two bastards set me up and got Chino killed," he said. "How can you explain that," he continued. Ant Love could see the heat blazing in King's eyes.

After King had left his early morning meeting, he went home and figured a few things out. He knew Ant had to be involved. He was the only person who knew about the drop off location. So it made it clear that he was the mole. However, seeing Kadijah, Chino's girlfriend, naked in Ant's bed was a total surprise to King.

"What do you want me to do with this dirty whore," Zeta asked King? "Let her visit Chino," he replied. Zeta aimed her pistol at Khadijah and unloaded her .38 into her head and body. She slumped back into the bed. As she lay in a pool of her blood, her spirit began to transition.

"Look, man, it was Vance who had yall setup," Ant Love said in a scared voice. He sat next to Khadijah's lifeless body and was terrified with each glance.

"No nigga, you and Vance set me up," King said. "Man, fuck this traitor," Biggie snapped. "This nigga got

Chino killed," Biggie said keeping his aim steadied at Ant's head.

"Where's my product," King asked. "It's under the bed. But I only have fifty kilos, Vance has the rest! Please don't kill me, King, I can help you get Vance back. I have his number and info on his meet up spots." Ant Love pleaded.

Biggie grabbed Ant Love's cell phone from off of his nightstand. He noticed written on a piece of paper there was a number with the letter V beside it, and an address of a car garage on Ridge Avenue.

"We don't need this traitor, I got it, King," he said, before placing Ant Love's cellphone and the paper inside of his pocket. "Not once did I ever do you wrong! But you go behind my back and betray me for a 100 keez. And because of your betrayal my godbrother lost his life. Shooting you ain't good enough, I want your snake ass to suffer and die slow," he said.

Zeta and Biggie duct taped Ant Love's mouth and tied up the naked body. They then wrapped him up with the bloodstained sheet before forcefully tossing him in the back of Biggie's van; along with the 50 kilos.

As they headed to West Philly, King made a call. His good friend was patiently awaiting their arrival. Face had introduced him to this man a few years earlier, but before today, King had only needed his services once. He was the best at what he did and today King was in need of his one of a kind treatments.

Twenty minutes later the van pulled up in front of a small row house. A creepy looking, middle aged white man came outside. He wore a white doctor's lab coat.

"He's all yours Doc," King said, as he watched Doc lick his lips. "Do what you want but take your time with him," King demanded.

LATER THAT NIGHT
AT AN UNDISCLOSED LOCATION

Tito "Mad Man" Vasquez was the cocaine kingpin of New York City. He controlled all five boroughs, parts of Northern New Jersey and had ties to a small section of Philly. Tito was half Cuban and Colombian, and well-connected and respected throughout the drug underworld. He was associated with the Bloque Meta cartel in Colombia and the Cuban Mafia in Miami. Each month he received a large shipment of cocaine from his suppliers and had the drugs distributed in large U-Haul trucks to its east coast destinations.

Tito sat down beside Vance and looked deep into his eyes. "I don't trust many people, but you are one of the one's that I do trust," Tito said. "You've been very loyal, and you have also made me a ton of money. My cousin Rosa also thinks very highly of you."

Vance smiled and nodded his head, pleased to hear the praise. As he listened to Tito, he looked around at all the armed men surrounding them. The building was heavily guarded and protected by a state-of-art surveillance system. Vance noticed every twenty or so minutes a large U-Haul truck would enter, and another one would exit.

After their meeting had concluded, Tito walked Vance out the back door to his Range Rover.

"Your shipment will be there in the morning, my friend. Take care and I will see you again next month," Tito said extending his right hand. "For sure," Vance replied.

After they had shaken hands, Tito watched as Vance got into his Range Rover and his driver pulled off into the darkness of the night. Tito turned and walked back into his warehouse, clueless that there was a set of eyes watching, and recording his entire conversation.

As the Range Rover pulled on Interstate 95, heading back to Philadelphia, Vance looked over to his driver with a big smile plastered on his face.

"Did you get that," Vance asked. "Yes, I got it all. I took notes on their entire set up. It should be real easy for the team to do what needs to be done."

Vance lay back in the backseat as the soulful voice of Marvin Gaye flowed through the speakers. He closed his eyes thinking of the money he was about to make as he drifted off.

XIX
KING OF PRUSSIA

King laid back on the sofa with his arms stretched behind his head, with his eyes closed. Again, Queen had his jeans down to his ankles. She was kneeled down, between his long legs, sucking every inch of his large, black dick. But, this time, her extraordinary performance was unlike any other time before.

King opened his eyes and watched as Queen slurped, licked and swallowed him whole. Her oral performance was epic. King had already cum twice, and he was still hard as a rock. Queen got up off of her knees and undressed. With one unzip she stepped out of her dress, and since she wasn't wearing a bra or panties, she stood perfectly sculpted in her birthday suit. King stared at his goddess as he desired to feel her insides.

"Are you ready to feel this good, wet, pink pussy," Queen asked. King nodded his head and smiled. It was what he had been waiting for.

"If I fuck you-you better not fuck another bitch! It's not negotiable. You need to be sure you're ready for this because I don't share," Queen said in complete seriousness. "Does that count for you as well," King questioned? "I only fuck one man at a time. Ain't nothing change," she said. "What about that friend you had," he asked? "Like I said, I only fuck one man at a time, and I want that man to be you." "Then there's no more to be said. I'm yours," King replied. "And I'm all yours," Queen said.

Queen climbed on top of King and straddled herself on top of his long, hard dick. She placed her arms around his neck and began to kiss King zealously. She rode his dick like an expert. Her pussy was a perfect fit for his dick and soaking wet. Queen fucked King with every muscle and bone in her body.

"Take your pussy Babe! Beat this pussy up," Queen demanded, as she began to cum and squirt all over his dick. King watched as Queen stood up and turned around. Her ass was perfectly shaped, and when he smacked it, the bounce was sexy. He quickly got up from the couch and turned her around so he could fuck her doggy style.

"I said take your pussy King! Fuck your Queen," she said. King thrust his long, thick, hard dick deep inside of her warm, juicy pussy. Each powerful stroke had her pussy vibrating, and she let out sex-filled moans throughout the room. "Whose Pussy Is It," King asked, smacking her ass in between strokes. "Whose Pussy Is This," he yelled out.

"It's yours, My King! All this Pussy is yours!!! I'm...I'm...I'm about to cum again," Queen shouted.

For the next few hours, King and Queen were engaged in a sexual warfare. Both had multiple orgasms. It was the best either had ever had, and it was worth the wait. But the wait was now over, and King and Queen now wanted it more than ever.

XX
EARLY THE NEXT MORNING

As King lay in bed beside Queen's soft, naked body, he reached over and grabbed his vibrating cell phone.

"Wassup Biggie," he asked? "King, we got a serious problem. Trouble's in critical condition up at Presbyterian Hospital," Biggie said. "What the hell happened," King said, as he stood up from the bed. "It's a long story. I'm at the hospital with Zeta, see you when you get here," Biggie said, before ending the call.

"Bae, what's wrong," Queen asked with sincere concern? "I'm not sure yet but I have to make a run," he said, staring at his beautiful woman. "Okay, well handle your business. I have to run some errands myself," Queen said, as she got up and walked towards the bathroom.

"Do you need a ride? I can have one of my boys drop you off," King asked? "No, no that's cool. I'm okay. Just handle your business and be safe, because I don't want anything happening to my King."

King walked over to Queen and gave her a soft kiss on the sweet, plump lips.

"Don't worry my Queen, I'll be okay. I'll see you later tonight for round four," King said, before smacking Queen on her ass.

After showering and getting dressed, King rushed out the door and got into Nas' Escalade. King's thoughts were running rampant as his cell phone started to ring.

"What's up, Doc?"

"Well, I would like to see you sometime today."

"Alright, later on, this evening. Some things have come up, and I have a lot of running to do."

"That's fine. Just know you're going to be very proud of me when you get here," Doc said giggling, before ending the call.

...

Forty minutes later King walked into the hospital. Inside, Biggie and Zeta were keeping an eye out for any unwanted visitors.

"What the hell happened," King demanded to know. "Trouble's drug house got blown up last night. Five people got killed, and two are in critical condition," Biggie said. "Is Trouble okay," he asked? "Right now he's in a coma, but both of his legs were blown off," Zeta said. "What, "King said, sickened to his stomach by the news. "That's right, man. Somebody threw two hand grenades at his spot. The shit is all over the news," Biggie replied.

King sat down in an empty seat outside of Trouble's hospital room. The drug game had quickly become a drug war, and the rising body count of his family and crew was not something he could get used to. Frustration boiled inside his veins.

For a moment, he closed his eyes and started to plan. This bloody game wouldn't end, but he had to protect his crew, his family and himself.

A tap on his shoulder brought him out of deep thought.

"Don't stress Homie, they're gonna get what's coming to them. They done started something and now we're going to end it," Biggie promised.

XXI
SAN JOSE, COSTA RICA

Inside his private villa, near the Caribbean Sea, Face watched as his wife, mother, and children enjoyed themselves as they play in the pool. His most loyal friend, Quincy, walked over and sat down beside him.

"What's the news today," Face asked, as he sat there drinking a Margarita. "It's gone from bad to worse," Quincy replied. "Chino was killed in a robbery and early this morning I got news that Trouble was blown up inside his house. He's in a coma and critical condition for now."

Face nodded his head in disbelief.
"So Chino is dead huh?"
"Yes and from what I hear his girlfriend had something to do with it."
"Did King take care of it?"
"Yeah, he handled his business. The girl is gone, and Doc has the guy who set it all up," Quincy replied with a smirk.

"What do you think about King's position," Face asked? "It's still yet to be determined. He's young and dealing with a lot on his plate. This life ain't never easy. You can give them the game, but they've got to live. The one thing I hope is that he don't try to be you. He has to run his race and the less he thinks about trying to be you, the better off he'll be. He's a good, thorough wise young man, but he has so much more to understand about this life.

When it comes to the money, he's on that. The connect loves him. He just needs to handle these street issues if he ever plans to have a long run in this game. The streets choose their champion, just like the streets chose you."

Face sat in total silence. King was his favorite little cousin and even though he didn't want to see him dead, he didn't want to interfere. King said he was ready; he said he wanted the throne; so Face had to wait it out.

"Thanks, Quincy, I appreciate you. Keep me updated."

"Always, "Quincy said as he stood up and walked away.

...

"Fuck that nigga! Like I said Vance is going to pay for what he did to my wife," Plex said, as he stared at a silver urn that held his wife's ashes. His friend Bobby stood in silence as he watched Plex vent out his anger.

"I'm going to catch him slipping one day soon. He's caught up in a drug beef with King's organization and he ain't worried about me. He got more on his plate than he needs and I'm just waiting for my moment. Soon as his bitch ass slips I'll be there," Plex said, kissing the final resting place of his beloved wife.

XXII
BALA CYNWYD, PA

Vance stood behind the door of his lavish home holding his loaded .357. He heard someone turning the doorknob and quickly grabbed his gun. The home security system had been disabled after a recent storm, leaving the perimeter cameras dysfunctional. As soon as the individual entered the home they were greeted with a loaded gun to the dome.

"Daddy it's me," the female voice yelled out. "Queen, why the hell you ain't call me first? I almost blew your damn head off," Vance said, before giving Queen a hug. "So where the hell have you been at? You usually check in but now you're too grown to come home sometime. And how much you need this time?"

Vance walked over to the sofa and sat down on the couch with his daughter. Queen and her father, Vance, had a strange relationship. Unlike his younger daughter, Kristen, Queen, was the daughter birthed by his mistress. His mistress was a former stripper, named Sunshine, who died mysteriously ten years earlier.

After the death of her mother, Queen moved in with her father. From day one the two could not get along, and it was obvious that Queen had some animosity towards her father. They had a love-hate relationship, but at the end of the day, they were family.

"I've been focused on getting my life in order. Ain't that what you told me to do? And I don't need any of your money," Queen said proudly. "And just so you know I have a new man, and we're good," she said. "Oh really? Well, I hope this new boyfriend of yours will treat you better than your last one did," her father said. "He don't beat on me like Mark did if that's what you're asking. He is a real man so you won't have to interfere this time," Queen replied.

Queen looked at her father's devilish grin and just shook her head. After her father had learned that Mark was putting his hands on her, his lifeless body turned up in Fairmount Park with six large bullet holes blown through it.

"So, who is this new guy and when can I meet him?" "He's a very private man and right now that's how I'm going to keep our relationship. Private! I don't want any family interference," Queen replied.

Vance looked Queen deep into her eyes and said, "I'm your only family and don't you ever forget that!"
"You're my only family, so why don't you act like it? Why do I feel like an outcast, like an unwanted child of yours that you had by one of your whores? You say you love me, but all you ever did for me was give me money. And you kept me away like I was a secret child you were ashamed of!"

Vance sat quietly as Queen continued to vent.

"Tell me, Dad, what happened to my mother? Why don't you ever talk about that?"
"It's not too much to talk about because I can only tell you what I know. Someone poisoned your mother, that's all I know," Vance replied.

Queen gave her father her familiar look when she was dissatisfied with his answer. She knew he wasn't going to say any more than he had already said for the past several years. However, she knew he knew more than he had said. He wasn't the type not to be informed.

"So do you like this new guy," Vance asked, changing the subject? "No. I love him. He's my new king and, this time, I found a man that respects me, speaks to me like the queen I am, and he'd never put his hands on me."

Vance grabbed Queen's hands and looked into her ever-changing light eyes and said, "If you feel that way about this guy then always remember, don't let anyone come between you two. If this is the man, you want to build your future with, then be committed to him. Respect him and don't bring your baggage to what you're building. Maybe one day I'll have the privilege to meet him."
"Hopefully," Queen said, as she stood up.

"So where are you staying now," Vance asked. "I'm good Dad. Don't worry. When I need to I'll reach out to you, and I'll call before I come the next time," she said, touching her head. "Okay. And yeah do that," Vance said, walking Queen to the door. "Oh hold up. I have something for you," Vance said, as he walked down into the basement.

Moments later Vance came out of the basement holding a small box.

"It's some of your mom's belongings. I meant to give it to you for some time now."

Queen took the box and said, "Thanks, Dad! I'll call you soon, and I'll be back when I get some free time."

Vance kissed Queen on the cheek and watched as she walked away and got into her car. At the same time, a gray Ford pulled up in the driveway and two white men exited the car. Queen knew the men had to be law enforcement agents just by their demeanors.

After watching the men go into her father's house, Queen pulled off. She glanced over at the box which held her deceased mother's belongings. Sadness instantly swept through her body, and her tears begin falling.

XXIII
CLUB ONYX

The established gentlemen's club was packed with strippers, hustlers and ballers. Flashing lights lit up the club like it was the 4th of July. Stacks of dollars, bottles of Cîroc and Henny were everywhere, as two attractive strippers performed a sensual dance act on the pole as if they were trained Olympic gymnasts. The DJ had the music banging, playing the newest party jams by Drake, Chris Brown, and Future.

Tasty noticed a familiar face as soon as he walked through the doors. It was Toney, one of the top guys from Vance's drug organization. She had gotten a few pictures of him from Zeta, and she was positive it was him. As soon as Toney sat down Tasty was on him. She could see in his lustful eyes that he liked what he saw. Her body was on point, and her face was flawless.

"What's up handsome," she said, climbing on top of his lap. "Yo wassup sexy," he said rubbing on her legs. "Oh is that right," Tasty said, applying her charm and rubbing up against his hard dick.

Toney ordered a thousand dollars in one dollar bills and a bottle of Pineapple Cîroc. For the next hour, Toney and Tasty enjoyed themselves in a private booth. She flirted, touched, licked and teased Toney enough to make him lust after her.

"So what do you want to enjoy the rest of your night with me," Toney asked. "A stack and I will give you a night you'll remember for the rest of your life," Tasty replied, as she licked her lips with her long, appealing tongue.

"Where do you live," he asked? "West Philly. I stay at the West Park housing projects," Tasty lied. "Okay, yeah I'm familiar," Toney said. "Can you wait for me till I get off? That way we can be straight about our business, "Tasty asked? "Pretty, I sure will. I'll be parked in the front," he said. "What are you driving, so I know what car to bring my wet pussy too," she said, placing his finger close to her kitty.

"I'm in a silver S550 Mercedes," Toney grinned. "Okay, I'll meet you out front. I have to make my rounds, and then I'll change real quick, and I'll be ready," Tasty said before she kissed him on his left cheek and walked away.

Tasty rushed to the employees stations and called Zeta

"I'm bringing him to the spot," Tasty said. "Okay. Good job Boo. I'll see you shortly," Zeta replied.

In his private customer's room, Toney was enjoying another lap dance, but he couldn't get Tasty off his mind. His hard dick wouldn't let him and he couldn't wait to bust his load off all over her sexy body.

XXIV
WEST PHILLY

Inside Doc's basement King, and Biggie stood back with stunned expressions on their faces. They had heard the rumors and horror stories about Doc. He was known for being a man to help poor folks who couldn't get traditional medical care, but he was legendary for torturing, mutilating and murdering people.

Doc was one person in the small group of people that King's cousin, Face, trusted with his life. After getting kicked out of medical school, Doc had taught himself everything about the human brain and body. Inside his dungeon of doom were walls full of computers and stacks of books about brain surgeries, the human heart, and more.

On the surface, Doc was unsuspecting and seemed kind and caring. However, underneath his passive personality, he was a stone cold, psychotic, sociopathic killer. He had killed several dozen people and eaten many of them as well. Cannibalism was his specialty, a delicacy for the doctor. He craved the taste of human flesh and eyeballs were a treat he could never get enough of.

Ant Love's naked body was strapped to a vertical table. His hands had been removed, along with his ears and penis. Doc had also detached his eyes and tongue.

"Damn what did you do with all his body parts," Biggie asked? Doc looked at Biggie with a devilish grin on his face and said, "I ate them." Then he licked his lips.

"King, Face told me to look out for you whenever you were in need, and I will," Doc said. King and Biggie watched in horror as Doc walked over to Ant's disfigured body and started to lick all over it.

"This is some of my best work," he said, before wiping the blood from his lips. "I'll be enjoying this fellow for the next month or so. Right now you might not believe it, but this fellow is still alive. But, he won't last too much longer."

King looked at his vibrating cell phone. It was an emergency call from Zeta.

"We've got to go Biggie. Thanks, Doc," King said.

Doc walked them back upstairs and to the front door. "I'm here whenever you need me," Doc said before closing the door behind them.

"Man that dude is fucking crazy," Biggie said. He scares the shit out of me, and I'm never scared. Had me thinking he might start eating my little black ass! Now I see why Face kept his scary ass in the tuck. He do know how to handle some shit, but damn," Biggie said as they got into Nas' Escalade.

"We got one," King said to Biggie. Biggie pulled out his Glock 17 and smiled. "They take one of ours; we take ten of theirs," Biggie said. "That's right," Nas said, as he drove down Lancaster Avenue.

...

Queen pulled over to the side of the road so she could check her incoming text message.

Hey, Babe, I'm running a Lil late. Can you go to my apartment and wait there for me?

She responded:
Yes, King, I'll be there waiting. Oh, and I have a surprise for you

Love Queen.

Queen looked over at her friend and said, "It's on tonight. I need you to be on your A-game."
"Don't worry, I will be," the woman said.

XXV
BALA CYNWYD, PA

Vance walked the two white men to the front door.

"Thanks for everything Vance, we will get on this as soon as possible. Remember, the more information we get, the better," one of the federal agents said. "See you soon," his partner added.

Vance watched as the two federal agents got into their unmarked car and drove off. Vance sat back down on his sofa and put his legs up on the coffee table. Then he lit up a Cuban Cigar as he relaxed on his comfortable couch.

Vance had a secret that only a few had known. He had a very private, top-secret file within the bureau and he was a prized informant. For nineteen years Vance had been an undercover street informant for the FBI. As long as he provided the FEDS with reliable information they could use to get indictments or convictions, they let him run his drug organization without any disruptions. They overlooked the many kidnappings and murders he had piled up because Vance's information had led to over one-hundred convictions with the Italian Mafia, the Russian, the Chinese mobsters, and the Dominican drug cartels. And fifteen years ago he had tried to set up Face, but he never got a hold of any reliable information.

In his lavish home, Vance sat alone puffing on his Cuban. With the FEDS on his team, he had been untouchable for almost 20 years. Unbeknownst to everyone around him, Vance was one of the biggest rats in the city.

XXVI
WEST PARK HOUSING PROJECTS

On the corner of 46th and Market Streets, sat the West Park Housing Projects. They were known for violence, drugs, and poverty.

Tasty and Toney stepped off the elevator when it reached the 19th floor.

"I've wanted you all night," Toney said, smacking her ass. "Then I hope you can show me because I'm overdue for some good dick. My toy just ain't cutting it anymore," Tasty said, as she took out her key and opened up the door.

When they stepped inside Toney noticed the well-decorated home. Even though they were in the projects, the apartment was well furnished and looked as if it had come straight out of the pages of Philadelphia Magazine.

"I'll be right back handsome. You can get relaxed," Tasty said, before walking into the back room. Toney grabbed the remote control and turned on ESPN. Moments later Tasty walked out with nothing on.

"Whatchu waiting for? Are you ready to beat this pussy up or not?"

Toney jumped up and immediately begin to undress. In less than a minute he was standing butt-ass naked, with his rock hard dick sticking out like a tree branch. Toney followed Tasty into the dimly lit bedroom, and they laid across the large King size bed.

"Hold up one minute. I need to use the bathroom," she told him, before getting up and walking out of the room.

Suddenly the door burst open. Biggie, Zeta, and King rushed into the room, pointing guns at Toney's head. At that moment, Toney knew he had been set up by Tasty. And the worst part was that he had left his gun in his jacket pocket that was in the living room.

"Damn that bitch got me," Toney yelled.

Tasty walked back into the room, fully dressed. "Yup, you trick ass nigga! Thanks for the two grand and rule number one, never trust a bitch that you just met in a strip club." "Fuck you bitch," Toney shouted. Zeta smacked him hard with her .38 special. "No, fuck you, nigga!"

Toney wiped the blood from his mouth and said, "Is this about money? How much? I'll make one call and get yall whatever you need in less than an hour."

King didn't like Toney's demeanor or his cocky attitude.

"So this is a game to you, huh," King said. "You think killing Sammy, Chino and blowing up my drug house was cute?"

Toney heard the sternness in King's voice and quickly changed his tune. "Look, man, it's all part of the game. You would've done it to us. That's what war looks like," he said. "You're right. Get up," King ordered him.

"Can I put my clothes on?"

"No motherfucker just get up or die right here," Biggie told him.

They walked Toney out of the apartment and towards the stairs that led to the roof of the nineteen-story building. King pushed Toney to the edge of the roof as he pressed his loaded 9mm against his back.

"Please man please don't kill me! It was Vance and Terry! I'm just a worker," he said, pleading for his life. Toney was afraid to look down because he had always been afraid of heights.

"Please God! Please, God, don't let me die like this," Toney yelled out.

King told Toney to turn around and face him. He looked into Toney's eyes and said, "God can't save you right now, only a net." Then King pushed him off the edge of the roof. They all watched as Toney fell nineteen stories. Toney's naked body splattered all over the cold pavement below. There was no denying it; he was dead.

"Get me his cell phone and Tasty you can keep whatever money he's got in his pocket," King said, as they walked back inside the building. Twenty-five minutes later, Zeta had driven Toney's Mercedes in the back of Overbrook High School, and Tasty followed. There it was doused with gasoline and set on fire.

COTTMAN & THE BOULEVARD
NORTHEAST PHILLY

Plex was sitting inside his car talking to his friend, Bobby. A loaded AK-47 lie across his lap.

"Man you ready to get up out of here and go back home," Bobby asked as he started yawning. "No! I'm going ride by every one of Vance's old hangouts until I find him," Plex snapped.

Bobby saw that Plex was obsessed with killing Vance. He couldn't eat, drink or sleep, without thinking about the demise of his nemesis, Vance. Plex was serious about his mission, and no one could change his mind.

Bobby sat back and listened while Plex voiced his frustrations. He knew it was best to remain silent and wait for Plex to tell them their next move.

5TH & TIOGA STREETS
NORTH PHILLY

As the tinted black Range Rover pulled in front of the Papi store, Vance stepped out of the car holding a large Adidas sports bag. The rundown Puerto Rican community was a known drug environment and authorities never did much to slow down the flux of drugs that invaded the neighborhood.

Two Puerto Rican men greeted and escorted Vance inside the store and down the basement. Vance ordered his driver to remain in the truck.

"Wassup Pedro, you're finally ready to do this and be a part of the winning team," Vance said, opening the bag up. "It's all there Pedro. The work, the grenades and two assault rifles. Just as you asked."

Pedro inspected the merchandise and was pleased. Vance and Pedro had known each other for a while and had done a few minor business deals in the past. A year earlier Pedro's cousin, Raul, had introduced them. Raul was currently serving time at Curran-Fromhold Correctional Facility (C.F.C.F.) on State Road. He was busted for a drug charge, but he lawyered up and was fighting the charges.

"Everything looks good," Pedro said, before passing Vance a backpack filled with cash. "No need to count it, it's all there," Pedro said. "I believe you. Call me when you need me again," Vance said, on his way up the stairs.

Pedro and his friend followed behind Vance. As they got to the front door, they watched as Vance walked towards his car. Plex and Bobby were driving pass and spotted Vance getting into his Range Rover.

"Yo, that's Vance! Pull over," Plex shouted. Bobby pulled over slowly and watched Vance enter the vehicle. "Easy. Let them go ahead of us but don't lose them."

The narrow street was too small for a drive-by. Besides, Plex did not want to shoot anyone but his intended target so he made the decision to follow Vance.

As Plex wrote down the truck's license plate, a police car pulled behind Bobby's car.

"Stay calm Bobby and keep following that Range Rover," Plex demanded.

At the corner of 9th and Luzerne Streets, the Range Rover drove through a fast-changing yellow light. Bobby was stuck at the red light with the cops behind them.

"Fuck! Fuck! They got away," Plex angrily shouted. "Well, at least, you got the license plate number," Bobby replied. Plex was disappointed because at that moment he wanted much more than those license plate numbers.

XXVII
LINCOLN GREEN APARTMENTS
CITY LINE AVENUE

As King walked into his apartment, he heard the familiar sounds of sexual pleasure escaping the confines of his bedroom. Perplexed, he slowly crept towards the room as he reached for his handgun. When he pushed the door open, he was pleasantly surprised to gaze upon this quixotic view.

Queen's legs were spread wide apart as she lay on the bed while a beautiful Latin woman sucked and licked on her pussy. Queen continued to enjoy the oral pleasures she received while King stood there in the doorway watching. The more he had learned about Queen, the more he craved her.

"So, are you just going to stand there with a hard dick or are you going to join my girlfriend and me? Her name is Sofie, and she wants to taste you," Queen said as the sexy woman looked up and smiled at King.

King started to undress in the doorway as he stared at Sofie's impressive body. She was beautiful. Her long dark brown, wavy, hair hung midway down her back, and her full C cup breast was perfectly round and firm.

Sofie noticed King's dick and her eyes lit up. "Wow Papi, you gonna have to take it easy on me with that thing."

King walked over and joined the two attractive women on the bed. For the next few hours, he fucked, licked, kissed, ate, smacked, choked, and spanked the two willing participants. This experience was King's first ménage a trios, and if Queen was willing, it would not be his last.

EARLY SATURDAY MORNING
LAWNCREST CEMETERY

King, along with members of his family and friends, stood watch as Robert "Chino" Smith was laid to rest. A lonely tear fell from King's eyes. He could not believe he was burying his godbrother and first cousin.

After the dirt was positioned over Chino's casket, King walked his Aunt Pattie to her limousine. She looked him in his watery eyes and said, "You make sure whoever killed my only son pays for this! King, you promise me that!"

Her words caused King to choke up. He fought back his tear as he said, "I promise you, Aunt Pattie." His distraught aunt said, "I know you will do this for me. His mother should feel exactly what I'm feeling. An eye for and eye, King. Give me my peace, son."

They hugged, but no further words exchanged. His aunt had made it clear she wanted revenge, and King knew what he was being asked to do.

XXVIII
ROSE HILL CEMETERY

On the opposite side of town, Vance, Terry, Carvin, and a few others attended the burial of Terry's twin brother, Jerry Lucas. Instead of the traditional black attire, at Terry's request, everyone wore white suits.

For most of the day, Terry was silent. Anger, rage, and frustration plagued him. Terry could have never imagined this day, and the pain he endured was crippling.

Once the burial ended, Vance and Terry stayed behind as the fleet of white Mercedes limousines drove off. Terry walked over to his brother's eternal resting place and broke down. He could no longer hold in the pain. His nose ran like a broken faucet, and Terry wept like a baby.

Vance could say nothing to calm Terry, so at that moment he did the best thing anyone could do for a friend; let him grieve. Only time would heal the gaping hole in Terry's heart and then again some losses are unrepairable.

LATE THAT EVENING
CHESTER, PA

King parked his car in front of a large warehouse. His bodyguards, Nas and right-hand man, Biggie, were already there waiting for him. A brown skin man opened the door to the warehouse and let them inside.

"Wassup Haze is everything good," King asked as he walked in. "Yeah Bossman, the weapon's shipment, and coke came in about an hour ago, Haze replied.

King and Biggie walked over to a row of refrigerators, washers, dryers, and dishwashers. King opened up one of the refrigerators and saw the neatly stacked packages of pure cocaine.

As they checked the contents of the appliances, a tall, dark-skinned man walked into the warehouse and approached King. Mike Thompson was a veteran detective with ten years in on the Philadelphia Police Force. For the past year, he had been on King's payroll.

"Wassup Mike, what did you find for me," King asked. "Nothing! I can't seem to find anything concrete on Vance. It's very strange. The only things I've been able to get are his records about the trials. Nothing new is coming up. His records are hidden pretty well. However, I did find out that his lawyer; James McDuffie was a former agent of the FBI. Maybe there's a connection somewhere there, but he's not in the FBI, ATF, or DEA database. It's like Vance is a ghost but something is strange when the FEDS don't have records on a known drug kingpin."

King looked at Mike and said, "Just keep looking, something will hit the surface."

XXIX
INSIDE A HOUSE
17ᵀᴴ & DIAMOND STREETS

"This is so fucked up," Terry said. "Now we have to bury Toney in a few days," he continued. "It's a part of the game, but I promise you I'm going to get to the bottom of this," Vance said. "What the hell was he doing on the roof, though, I thought he said he was going down Onyx," Carvin said.

"Toney was set the fuck up! There's no way he jumped off a nineteen-story building! That nigga wasn't suicidal," Terry shouted in frustration.

Vance sat at the table putting his thoughts together. His friend, Toney, was found naked and dead; and the cops had no suspects.

"Terry, you and Carvin go by Onyx and see if Toney was kicking it with one of them nasty ass strippers. Maybe he left with one of them, and they had something to do with this," Vance said. "I'm on it," Terry said, as he and Carvin got up from the table and left the house.

Ten minutes later two white Federal Agents pulled up and parked their car. Vance opened the door for them as they came inside and sat down.

"What do you have for us Mr. Lewis," one agent asked. Vance pulled out a small tape recorder and a backpack with over two hundred thousand inside of it.

"I sold seven kilos to Pedro, yesterday and I got the buy recorded. He also purchased two military assault rifles and the two hand grenades Y'all gave me."

"Wonderful job Vance! We have been trying to get a big buy on Pedro for the past six months, "the agent said enthusiastically.

Vance looked at the two agents and said, "Just make sure this dude pleads out like all the others!"

"Don't they all? They either plead out for lesser time and some come play on our team, just like you. Vance, you don't have to worry. We have a 98% conviction rate because we know how to do our jobs. Pedro Gonzalez is looking at life. This is his third felony," the agent replied.

"He didn't mention anything about the drugs or the exact amount of money on tape, did he," one of the agents asked. "No, we only talked about the guns and grenades. If not just edit the tapes like Y'all usually do," Vance replied. "Good. Then the money is ours. Keep up the good work," he said, passing Vance fifty grand in cash.

Vance walked the agents out and watched as they drove away. Vance felt no shame although he had become the thing he once despised, a snitch. Like most drug dealers, he hadn't lived by the code for some time. His loyalty was to himself and no one else. He was the worst kind of man; a man with no morals and no respect for the game.

Men like Vance had turned a game of honor among hustlers, into who will snitch first. The 70's, 80's, and early 90's were long gone. Ever since new federal drug laws and regulations had passed in 1992, drug dealers were singing more than church choirs were.

Vance sat on the couch shifting through his Federal Donation Fund. Then he lit up a Cuban Cigar and enjoyed the taste of his favorite pastime.

CITY LINE AVENUE

"Are you okay," Queen asked King as they lay together in bed. "You've been distant all day."

King looked at Queen and said, "I have something to tell you." Queen saw the seriousness in King's eyes and then placed her finger on his lips.

"What, do you want to confess finally that you're a drug dealer?" King was surprised. "How did you..." Queen interrupted him. "I've been around. I am not stupid King. The cars, the condos, the money, jewelry, oh and you've got a bodyguard. All you have to do is watch. But you better be glad I'm not a cop, or I would have to lock your ass up," Queen joked.

King was silent as Queen went on.

"I don't know how big you are, but I do know you're an important player. I've been around my share of players and bosses." "Is that right, "King asked? "Yes. I grew up around men who were bosses," Queen said, as she rolled over on King's chest.

"Do you want to know what's been on my mind all day," King asked. "Yes, I do. Is it Chino's funeral that's been troubling you," Queen said. "Follow me," King said getting up from the bed.

Queen followed King over to the closet door. The large walk-in closet held their expensive clothing and shoes. Queen waited while King pulled out an all-white Burberry dress and a pair of white Christian Louboutin pumps and handed them to her. She was excited to receive the new gifts and could not wait to try them on.

Queen rushed to try on her dress, but King pulled her hand and asked her to wait. Then he reached into the left pocket on a pair of his pants. He pulled out a small white box. Queen trembled. King then got down on one knee and opened the box holding a platinum, five-carat princess cut ring.

"What I want to ask you is if you'll be my wife," King said, as Queen dropped to her knees. "Yes, I would love to be your wife," Queen said, as tears of joys trickled from her eyes.

XXX
ONE MONTH LATER

King and Queen were married in a small ceremony in Conshohocken, PA. Only his closest family members and friends were invited. Queen decided she didn't want any of her family members to attend. King was now all the family she wanted and needed, and no one would come between them.

The couple hadn't had years to get to know one another, but their love was evident to everyone in their presence. They were connected spiritually and had profound respect for each other.

After the wedding, King and Queen boarded one of Face's private jets and flew to the island of Aruba. The newlyweds were headed on a honeymoon filled with shopping, eating, partying, and endless hours of lovemaking.

5:45 A.M.
PHILADELPHIA, PA

A swarm of FBI and ATF agents surrounded the two-story building, and within moments, a military style tactical team forcefully entered the building. With infrared guns aimed, they swept the building. Upon entering a back bedroom, they saw Pedro Gonzalez lying in bed with two exotic Latin women. With a look of disbelief plastered on his face, all he could do was shake his. The FEDS abruptly ended his ten year run in the game.

Pedro was handcuffed and read his Miranda rights, before being rushed downtown to the federal detention center.

Pedro sat alone in his cell, and his mind roamed. He tried his best to come up with a plausible reason as to why he was now behind bars. His organization had been airtight for a decade, and he had always been overly cautious. Pedro thought about any new people he had recently made connections with.

"This can't be true," he whispered to himself. "Vance can't be a snitch it has to be someone else. "

Pedro laid back on his cot and placed his hands behind his head. He was determined to find out who was the informant on his case. Pleading out was not an option, Pedro lived by the old code. Whoever was the snitch Pedro, wouldn't rest until he or she was exposed. He figured once he linked up with his lawyer he would know who was behind his arrest.

In the silence of his cell, Pedro lay still on his cot. "Fuck the FEDS! I'm going to expose this fucking rat," he said.

BALA CYNWYD, PA

Once a month, Vance's youngest daughter, Kristen, came to the house for weekend visits. Eleven-year-old Kristen was brilliant and spoiled. She enjoyed shopping, hanging out with friends, watching her favorite television shows and posting pictures on her social media. Kristen was addicted to Facebook, Twitter, and Snapchat, but her favorite was Instagram. Throughout the day she scrolled down her Instagram timeline, posting multiple pictures of herself as part of her daily routine.

Vance walked into the living room. Kristen sat in front of the large television and played on her iPhone. His youngest daughter was the apple of his eye, and she could do no wrong. Vance spoiled her and anything she asked for appeared quicker than a genie could grant a wish.

This young child's wardrobe surpassed most adults and with Gucci, Chanel, Prada, Louis Vuitton, Burberry, and Tori Burch at her fingertips she could easily out dress most celebrities. Kristen also loved jewelry, and her diamond earrings, watches, and necklaces were insured for more than a half-million dollars.

Vance blessed his youngest with a perfect life. Kristen was enrolled in private school, had a million-dollar trust fund set aside for her once she turned twenty-one, and besides Queen, she was set to inherit millions from his life insurance policy upon his demise.

"What are you doing, Baby," Vance asked. "I'm just posting pictures on my Instagram, Daddy." Vance smiled and then sat down on the sofa. As long as Kristen, was happy, he was happy.

Kristen continued to post pictures on Instagram, as her father dozed off on the couch.

XXXI
TWO DAYS LATER
OCTOBER 31ST

Inside Trouble's hospital room, King, Biggie, and Zeta stood beside his bed. The wounds he suffered were so severe that both legs were amputated, and his right hand had to be removed. King didn't have the words to describe his frustrations. Biggie was so disturbed after a few he had to leave the room.

"Don't worry I'll be alright yall," Trouble said. "We're going to get them Trouble," Zeta said. "I give you my word," she continued, as she kissed his cheek. Immediately she became overwhelmed with tears and left the room to join Biggie in the waiting room.

"Hey, man are you okay," Trouble asked.

"Shit, I should be asking you that. But I'm good, just trying to stay focused out here on the streets."

"How is married life treating you?"

"I'm enjoying it," King said with a smile.

"She's a good girl, a real rider. You got yourself a jewel with Queen."

"Just get well Homie and don't worry about nothing. All your bills are covered and soon as you're cleared to leave here we have a private rehabilitation center waiting on."

After leaving the hospital, King, Biggie and Zeta got into the waiting Mercedes. King sat in the front.

"What Y'all two up to? I see your faces," King said looking towards the backseat.

"We got some business to take care of," Biggie replied.

"And when is this?"

"Tonight," Zeta said, with a devilish grin.

"You ready Babe?" Queen said, sitting behind the wheel.

"Yes. Let's get out of here. I can't stand hospitals."

ON THE CORNER OF 23RD & TASKER

"We had that motherfucker! I don't know why I didn't just jump out of the car and hit that bitch ass nigga up," Plex shouted, as he sat inside of his car. Bobby remained silent. He had been in the car with Plex since seven in the morning, and they were still on the hunt to find Vance or The Twins.

"That nigga killed my wife," Plex said as he began loading his .45 caliber. "You know today is Halloween right," Plex asked. "Yes," Bobby replied. "Well then you know some fucked up shit gonna pop off today. I have a strange feeling about tonight."

Bobby nodded his head in agreement. He knew Plex was going through a lot of personal issues, and he didn't feel the need to say much. The hatred for Vance and his crew was written all over Plex's face, and his quest to find them was driving his friend crazy.

XXXII
HALLOWEEN NIGHT

Terry and one of his goons walked into the crowded gentleman's club. Tonight, Onyx was having a special event, hosted by female rap superstar, Nikki Minaj. The club was at capacity, and money and bottles were flowing everywhere.

This was Terry's second time at the club, and so far he learned Toney was last seen with a dancer who went by the name, Tasty. For a couple of dollars, any stripper in the club would tell him what he wanted to know. That's precisely what happened when Terry paid a stripper named Silver for information on Tasty. Silver was so forthcoming she even showed Terry photographs of Tasty from her Instagram page.

"That's her right over there," Silver said, as she pointed over to the VIP section. Terry grabbed Silver's hand and placed five one hundred dollar bills in it. "Do what you need to do and get her over here," he demanded.

Terry watched as Silver mingled, but quickly made her way through the boisterous crowd over to Tasty. Silver whispering in Tasty's ear and then pointing over to Terry. Moments later, Tasty walked up on Terry with a seductive look on her face. At first glance, he found her attractive and her body was enticing, but this visit was strictly business.

"I hear I'm your favorite dancer, and you've been looking for me," Tasty said. "Yup, you are," Terry said, pulling out a stack of hundred dollar bills. "Don't I know you from somewhere? Your face looks so familiar," Tasty said before she sat down on Terry's lap. "Maybe you've seen me around, but mostly I'm low key. But, what's up? Let's get out of here," Toney said. "Cute but tonight ain't good handsome. I can make a lot of money in here this evening. Plus, you ain't even tell me your name."

Terry looked straight into Tasty's eyes and said, "My name is Twin, and I will double what you make here tonight. I just need a few hours of your time." Terry then passed Tasty fifteen-hundred dollars. "You can get the other half after you show me what Tasty is all about."

Tasty was impressed. She knew real ballers when she came across them, and Twin was one. Besides, she was stacking her cash, so any bonus cash was exactly what she needed.

"Let's roll then," Tasty said. "Give me a few I have to change out of this outfit. I just hope you ain't crazy," she said jokingly. "There be a lot of crazy ass weirdoes coming in here," she continued. "No worries, Hun. I'm just trying to get to know the most beautiful woman I've seen in a long time." Tasty blushed and said, "Okay handsome, be back in fifteen minutes. I have to make up a lie or tell my boss something came up with my son."

Terry watched as Tasty walked away. Her ass is perfect, he thought. When Tasty walked into the locker room to change, she texted her girlfriend, Zeta.

Hey, Babe, I'm at the club. A new trick named Twin is paying me 3 grand for a little fun lol. I will be back in a few. Call you as soon as I get back.
Love You
Tasty

After pressing the send button on her iPhone, Tasty dressed quickly and rushed back to her handsome new trick. She was obsessed with money and three-thousand for an easy trick was right up her alley.

Ten minutes later they were inside of Terry's white BMW and headed towards North Philly. Tasty didn't know Terry's actual agenda, nor did she know his goon was following behind in a black truck.

WEST PHILLY

For the past hour, Zeta and Biggie sat inside of a stolen gray Toyota Camry across the street from a house on 52nd Street. It was Halloween night and plenty kids were out dressed in their Halloween costumes, clutching their goody bags filled with candy. They had silenced their cell phones to keep their focus on their current agenda.

A key source had given Biggie some valuable information on their mark. Their target had been right under their noses the entire time.

When a group of parents and unruly children walked up to the front door of the house and rung the bell, Zeta looked over at Biggie. "It's about that time," she said. Biggie reached under the driver's seat and pulled out a loaded 9mm and a green Incredible Hulk mask. He already had on the green body costume. Biggie placed his gun inside of a Trick-or-Treat bag, put on his mask, and then rushed out of the car. Biggie's short stature made it easy for him to blend in as one of the children who were out for Halloween.

Zeta watched as Biggie casually crossed the street. From the car she clutched her loaded .357 ready to make her move if necessary.

XXXIII
29ᵀᴴ & GIRARD
NORTH PHILLY

Tasty was impressed with the gorgeous layout of Twin's apartment.

"Get undressed," Terry told her. "Damn you don't play, huh," Zeta said, as she undressed. Terry sat back on the sofa and watched as Tasty stripped seductively. He was turned on, and Tasty could easily see the bulge in his jeans. When all of Tasty's clothes were off Terry stood up from the sofa and walked towards the bedroom.

"Remember, I want to be back at the club in an hour," Tasty said. "Lay on the bed," Twin demanded. Tasty heard the seriousness in Twin's voice and became uncomfortable. Her intuition told her something was wrong. She had known his face and when she realized who he was it was too late. A loaded .40 caliber was pointed at her head.

"What the hell is going on," Tasty said. "Shut up bitch and sit down!"

Terry passed Tasty a pair of handcuffs and said, "Put them on." She nervously did as told. Terry stood over Tasty and said, "If you lie you will never see your son again."

Tears started falling from Tasty's eyes. She knew she was in the presence of a homicidal monster. By the time she realized Terry was the same man Zeta had recently shown her a picture of, it was too late. He was one of the dreaded Lucas twins.

"Why did you set Toney up," he shouted. "Please! Please, I don't want no trouble. I have a four-year-old son," she cried out. "Bitch answer my damn question," he yelled. "It wasn't me, I swear," she pleaded.

Terry became irate. He coarsely threw Tasty on her stomach and pulled down his pants. Terry began to rape and sodomize Tasty. Then Terry called his goon into the room to join in. When they were done, Tasty's once beautiful face and body were severely bruised and battered. Blood ran down from her eyes, nose and mouth.

"I already know you work for King's organization! You and that bitch girlfriend of yours set up my Homie. Now you have to pay for your actions."

Terry placed the gun between Tasty's bloody eyes and squeezed the trigger. A piece of Tasty's brain flew across the bed.

"Cut this bitch up and clean this place up," Terry said to his goon as he started to get dressed.

WEST PHILLY

None of the children noticed Biggie as he calmly walked up the steps and joined them. He stood behind a short fat boy in a Spiderman costume. Carvin stood in the doorway handing out handfuls of candy, and his beautiful wife Gail stood beside him smiling.

Biggie pressed through the small crowd, pushing the kids out of his way to get closer to Carvin.

"Calm down Lil man you're going to get your candy," Carvin told the feisty trick-a-treater. Biggie reached inside the bag and swiftly pulled his 9mm. He pointed his gun at Carvin and opened fire.

"The Hulk is shooting at people," one of the children yelled out. The children and their parents panicked, as they screamed and ran away from the small gunman. Biggie continued to unload his weapon, shooting Carvin and his wife in their faces and chests.

When the massacre was over, Carvin and Gail's lifeless bodies lay next to each other encircled in a pool of blood. Biggie rushed back to his car, and Zeta quickly pulled off. As the darkness of the night concealed the two, they quickly got out of sight.

XXXIV
RITTENHOUSE SQUARE

Inside the elegant, five bedrooms, three-and-a-half bath, million dollar home, Face and King sat on the sofa conversing.

"You have to stay focused King and fix this mess!"

"I'm on it Face, but it's not as easy as it seems."

"I put the Empire in your hands, make me proud Lil Cuz."

"I will, I promise," King said.

"Now, what's up with this new wife of yours? Is she good?"

"She's better than good; she's one of a kind. I've never loved a woman as much as I love her."

"I need to see this woman who's got you on cloud nine."

"I'll be right back," King said, as he walked out of the house.

Moments later, King returned with Queen, wrapped in his arm. Face approved, and was very impressed with his cousin's beautiful new wife.

"So you're the Queen I keep hearing about?"

Queen blushed.

"Yes, I'm Queen, the one and only."

"Well, it's good to meet you. I'm Face."

"I know who you are," Queen said.

"You're a legend. How could I not know about you?"

"A legend. Thanks," Face said, as the trio sat down on the sofa.

After talking with Queen and King for almost an hour, Face undeniably was pleased with the couple. Queen was outspoken and strong willed. She reminded Face of a younger version of his wife, Tasha.

Before the couple left, Face said, "Make sure you take care of my Lil cousin." "Don't worry. That's easy, he's my King, so I got him covered," Queen said, before kissing Face on his left cheek. Face and King shook hands, and then Face gave Queen a hug as he walked them out of the door.

Returning to the sofa, Face, sat down to relax before making his next trip. He then opened the black briefcase King had bought him. Inside was a million dollars cash and a birthday card. The card read, *'Happy belated birthday– Love always your Lil cousin'*.

Face headed out the door, and he picked up the briefcase and placed it inside of the trunk. Then he got into the backseat of his waiting, black Maybach. The driver pulled off down the street, taking Face to his private jet at the Philadelphia International Airport.

NORTHEAST PHILLY

The black Range Rover pulled up and parked in the Walmart parking lot near the Roosevelt Boulevard. Moments later, a white van pulled beside Vance's Range Rover and parked. An enormous white man, standing around 6'5, and weighing a solid two-hundred-eighty pounds, got inside of Vance's truck.

"Wassup Vance," Victor said. "Wassup," Vance said, shaking the man's huge hand.

Victor Gavrikov was a cold blooded killer and one of the largest illegal arms dealers in America. For the past seven years, Victor had been living in the United States posing to be a legitimate business person. The truth was, Victor was a high-ranking member of the notorious Russian Mob. For three years, Victor and Vance secretly bought and sold illegal firearms and flooded the inner city streets with them.

Vance handed Victor a briefcase containing over four-hundred thousand in cash. They shook hands and Vance watched as Victor exited his car, and then walked near the entrance of the Walmart. Moments later, a black BMW pulled in front of Victor, and he got inside. Vance watched as the BMW sped off and disappeared into the cool, fall night.

Swiftly, Terry strolled from the Walmart and calmly walked over to a running van and jumped inside. As he pulled off, a Philadelphia Police car pulled behind him and began following the van.

Inside of Terry's vehicle was four-hundred dollars' worth of weapons and ammunition. And inside the police car was Sergeant John Carter, one of the most crooked cops on the force. His job was to ensure the shipment of guns were delivered to their destination, and so far he had always done his job.

MANAYUNK

Inside of her apartment, Zeta paced back and forth in the living room. She had called Tasty's cellphone over fifty times, and Tasty hadn't returned any of her text. Zeta knew something had gone seriously wrong.

Zeta called Tasty's job and was informed she had never returned after leaving out with an unknown male. Zeta looked over at Tasty's four-year-old son, Zack, who was asleep on the sofa. He too had been waiting for his mother to come home but grew tired of waiting and dozed off.

Zeta's worried eyes filled with tears. She tried to calm her nerves, but her fears of the certain fate her girlfriend had undergone wouldn't allow it.

Zeta walked back into the bedroom and turned on the television, as she laid across the bed. A Fox 29 News reporter appeared on the screen.

"Tonight has been one of the deadliest Halloween's in the City of Brotherly Love. Today, in West Philadelphia, the severed head of a young woman was found in the parking lot of Friday's restaurant, on City Line Avenue. Beside the woman's head was a copy of her Pennsylvania Driver's License. The women's name is Charlene Johnson, and she was a resident of the Lawncrest section of the city. Detectives are working round the clock to solve this murder, which has been added to the long list of unsolved homicides in the city"'

Zeta's screams ran through the apartment building. Her friend and lover for over three years was now gone. And just like her friend Sammy, Tasty's head had been removed from her body. This murder was identical to Sammy's.
It was another message being sent to King and his crew from Vance.

Zeta crawled into the corner and trembled uncontrollably. Her tears ran down her face like an overflowing river. She felt as if a piece of her heart and soul had been snatched from her chest. She began to feel numb as her breathing heavily increased. This was a pain she had never felt before.

Moments later, her bedroom door slowly opened, and little Zack ran over to Zeta.

"Don't cry Zee Zee, my Mommy will be home soon," he said, before lying across her lap. Zeta couldn't speak. She didn't have the words to explain to Zack that his mother was never coming home. How could she tell him about the awful way his mother had died? And how could Zeta not feel guilty for being unable to protect her girlfriend? Tonight she would hold the young boy as her tears fell, but there would be no words spoken.

WAYNE & CHELTEN AVENUE

Plex and Bobby parked in the Pathmark's Supermarket parking lot. Suddenly, they spotted the tinted black Range Rover they had been stalking, stopped at a red light.

"That's him," Plex said, as he put on a mask and grabbed the loaded AK-47 from off the back seat. Bobby drove out of the parking lot as fast as he could, and seconds later they were right behind the Range Rover.

When the light turned green, they followed closely behind. At the next red light, Bobby quickly pulled his stolen vehicle in front of the Range Rover, cutting it off. Without hesitation, Plex rushed out the car, holding his AK-47 and begin firing into the Range Rover.

Tat! Tat! Tat! Tat! Tat! Tat! Tat!
Everyone inside the vehicle was killed.

Plex quickly ran back into the car with Bobby. His adrenaline was racing, and they disappeared into the night.

Mistakenly, Plex and Bobby had just murdered the wrong people. Instead of killing Vance and one of his goons, he had killed an innocent father who was taking his son home after leaving a late night football practice.

XXXV
ONE WEEK LATER
STATE ROAD

Curran Fromhold Correctional Facility opened in 1995. Better known as C.F.C.F., it's the largest Philadelphia Prison System facility which consists of four housing buildings. The Correctional Facility was named in honor of Warden Patrick N. Curran and Deputy Warden Robert F. Fromhold, who were brutally murdered at Holmesburg Prison on May 31, 1973. The prison houses some of the most violent men from the Philadelphia area. For many, it is their temporary home while they await trial to fight murder and drug charges; before being sentenced and sent upstate.

Inside his cell, Raul Ortiz listened to Power 99 FM's, The Come up Show. It was the most popular rap station inside the prison. As he lay back with his eyes closed, he never saw the three Latin inmates rush into his cell. Each man was holding a sharp man-made shank.

Instantly, they pinned Raul down on his cot and begin savagely stabbing him. When they were finished, Raul's bloody corpse had received over one hundred stab wounds. Before the men left, they placed a small note on top of Raul's lifeless body that read: *Know your enemies before you introduce them to family.*

The note was a message from Raul's drug kingpin cousin, Pedro Gonzalez, who was currently at the Federal Detention Center (FDC), in downtown Philadelphia.

After meeting with his lawyer and reading his discovery, Pedro found out who was the government informant on his case. Now Pedro was left to prepare for his federal hearing that was scheduled in the upcoming weeks. Losing his case would mean a life sentence with no chance of parole.

Pedro sat in the Rec Room playing Domino with a few of his loyal men. A tall Black Muslim man walked over whispered, "It's done. Raul is sleeping with the rats," and then he walked off.

Pedro loved his younger cousin, but the mistake he made of trusting a Rat was unforgivable. Raul was supposed to have done his homework before introducing Vance to Pedro, and now the mistake had cost him his life.

As Pedro finished playing his game of Domino's, he sat contemplating on how he would get his revenge against Vance. He knew one of the best ways to kill a snitch was to expose him. If Vance were forced to take the stand, then there would be nowhere for him to hide, and the streets surely would have their way with that rat.

XXXVI
BALA CYNWYD, PA

When Queen pulled up and parked her new gold Lexus in front of her father's home, she saw two white men pulling off in a black Crown Victoria. Queen remembered the men from her last visit with her father.

"So what's the important news," Vance asked, Queen walked through the front door. After closing the door, Vance followed Queen to the sofa.

"Are you going to tell me what's wrong or not," Vance demanded. Queen looked into her father's eyes and then showed him her left hand. The stunning five-carat diamond ring instantly had his attention.

"You're engaged," he asked. "No Daddy. I'm married," Queen said proudly. "Married! Are you serious," he said surprised. "Yes, I'm very serious," Queen replied. "Well, I hope this new husband of yours is deserving of my daughter. And I guess I don't have to worry if he has enough money to sustain the type of life I want for you because from the size of that ring I can tell he's not struggling. So when do I meet this dude, "he asked.

"When I'm ready, Dad. Right now I don't want anyone, not even my father, messing in my personal matters."

Vance looked into his daughter's eyes and said, "That's fine with me, but if this so called king of yours is in the game, you better remember everything I taught you." "I know Daddy. I've paid attention, and you've been schooling me ever since I was a little girl," Queen said.

"Did your new king buy you that car too," Vance asked. "Yes, he did Daddy. All you need to know is he's taking good care of me. I don't want for anything," Queen said proudly.

Vance observed his daughter. She was beautiful, and he was very proud of the way she carried herself.

"If you need me, I'm here. Just be careful and stay safe." Queen stood up from the sofa and said, "I will Daddy."

Vance followed Queen to the door. Before she walked out, she asked, "Daddy, who were those white men I saw pulling off?" "Oh they're just a few business partners I've been working with," he lied. "Aren't they the guys you used to meet up with when I was a little girl," she said. "You remember that," Vance asked surprised. "Yes. You used to meet them at the supermarket," Queen said. "Yeah, that's them," Vance replied. "Wow, that's been over fifteen years ago. Must be some good business," Queen said, as she got into her car and pulled off.

XXXVII
34TH & HAVERFORD AVENUE
WEST PHILLY

Down in the basement of one of his stash houses, King watched as six naked females sat counting over a million dollars in cash. Stacks of bills, electronic counting machines, suitcases, and backpacks were in front of each woman. Standing beside King, were Biggie, Haze, and Zeta. A few feet away was King's bodyguard, Nas, listening to a police scanner. On the roof was another one of King's men. He watched for intruders through a pair of binoculars, while his Remington 700 sniper rifle lay directly beside him.

"Are you okay Zeta," King asked. "I'm good King, and thanks for paying for Tasty's funeral. You didn't have to, but it's appreciated, and that trust fund for her son was good looking out," Zeta said, becoming emotional as she was reminded of her recent loss. "It's the least I could do. She was a soldier, and she died for us," King said.

King placed his arm around Zeta and walked her to the back of the large basement.

"Zeta, I promise you we are going to handle this. Vance and his crew will not go unpunished, but I need you to stay level headed and don't do anything crazy. I don't want your temper getting you into trouble. Let's just stay focused and get them the right way," King said. "I'm good," Zeta replied.

King and Zeta walked back over to where Biggie was standing. "Y'all cool," Biggie asked. "We good," King said. "Yeah, we good," Zeta confirmed.

ROXBOROUGH

Plex pulled up and parked his car in front of Bobby's house. He started beeping the horn. Seconds later, Bobby walked out the front door and got into his car.

"You ready to go find this nigga," Plex said. "Man, I thought we were laying low for a while. We murdered the wrong people, man! Cops are out looking for us," Bobby said. "Fuck the cops! I'm not going to rest until I get them, niggas! They killed my wife, and the cops ain't do shit about it. So why should I care about who they're looking for! They don't know it's us, and I don't care if they do! I just want to get those niggas!"

Plex pulled down the street as his rage grew. He was determined on killing Vance and Terry. Nothing or no one could change his mind.

"Don't you feel any remorse for killing that man and his son?" Plex looked over at Bobby and said, "It's a war every day out here in these Philly streets. Sometimes there are casualties. That's just a part of life. And I don't feel shit but hate!"

XXXVIII
2:40 P.M.
TWO DAYS LATER

Queen pulled up and parked her Lexus in front of the Philadelphia Women's Center.

"Bitch, you know what you have to do," Queen said. Sofie looked over at her friend and said, "Queen, I'm so sorry about this. I took the Plan-B after we had sex that night, so I don't know what happened," Sofie cried. "Your ass got pregnant! That's what the fuck happened!"

Queen looked at her diamond Rolex watch and said, "Your appointment is at three-thirty. I'll be right here waiting for you when it's done. Now, go get rid of that shit before I get rid of it for you!"

Sofie got out of the car and sadly walked towards the entrance of the building. A part of her wanted to keep the child that was growing inside of her. In the twenty-seven years, she has lived, Sofie had never gotten pregnant. Although this wasn't planned, and certainly not an idea, she was now with child.

King had been the second man she had been sexually intimate with. Before King, she had been with women mostly. Sofie had an undeniable attraction to women. And when it came to Queen, Sofie was deeply in love with her. The two had been lovers for a few years.

As she got closer to the entrance, Sofie knew if she crossed Queen the consequences could be deadly. Sofie knew a side of Queen that was dark, scary, and lethal. As she continued to walk, Sofie contemplated her life changing decision.

THREE YEARS EARLIER
GERMANTOWN

Queen could hear fighting, screaming and yelling coming from the couple next door. She had seen the pair together a few times as they entered and exited the building. The female had been friendly and taken a liking to Queen. The women started spending time with one another; going shopping, out to eat, and hanging in each other's apartment when the woman's boyfriend wasn't home. What was supposed to be innocent, had turned into something else.

For a while, Queen and her neighbor had been involved in a secret lesbian affair. The two did their best to hide it. Many nights after her neighbor's boyfriend left for work; Queen called her female friend over. Their evenings were filled with pure and intense lovemaking. They craved each other's kiss and touch and often favored one another rather than spending time with a man.

Queen tried to ignore the distraction, so she turned up the volume on her television. She heard the constant screams from her lover as her boyfriend pounded his fist into her face. The fighting became too much to ignore.

Queen stood up from her sofa and ran into her bedroom. She reached under the mattress and pulled out a loaded .38 pistol. Then she rushed out of her apartment and went next door.

"Who the fuck is it," the male screamed, responding to the banging at his door. As soon as he opened the door,

Queen aimed her gun and shot the man twice; striking him in the head.

Sofie was stunned as she watched his lifeless body slump to the floor. Queen rushed into the apartment and dragged the body into the living room.

"Are you going to help me get rid of this assholes body or not," Queen said, sending Sofie, running to the bedroom to get a blanket. When she returned, Queen started wrapping the body inside of the dark colored blanket. Then Sofie helped Queen carry the body into the backseat of Queen's car.

Twenty minutes later, they were in a dark, secluded section in Fairmount Park. Sofie stood back and watched as Queen, doused the body with gasoline. Then she lit a match and threw it onto the body. They watched as the flames engulfed and scorched the corpse.

While riding back to the apartment, Queen looked at Sofie and said, "This is between us." Sofie replied, "I promise you. It is." Queen smiled and said, "You're mine now."

From that day, Sofie had pledged herself to Queen. Queen had been her personal savior. They had each other's back and had supported one another through pain and heartache. And both would take their deadly secret to the grave.

THE FEDERAL DETENTION CENTER

Inside the small private conference room, Pedro was sat at a small round table talking to his attractive female lawyer. JoAnn Morgan was one of the top criminal defense lawyers in the Tri-State. Her record was flawless, and she had a reputation for getting her clients off.

"Are you sure this is what you want to do, Mr. Gonzalez? "I'm positive. I want to take my case to trial. I want to expose Vance's snitch ass to everyone! He is a rat!" "But if you lose you're looking at a life sentence. Right now the government is offering you twenty years if you take the plea agreement." "Fuck the government! They support all these rats! They take care of informants, snitches, but hang all the loyal, stand up men that won't sing! Fuck THEM! I'm going to trial and can't nobody change my mind!"

JoAnn looked at the sternness inside of her client's eyes and shook her head in defeat before speaking.

"I will notify the Federal Prosecutor and tell them about your decision. On another note, did your sleeping conditions get any better inside of here," she asked. "No, I'm still up all night. It's too hard to sleep in here, and they won't let medical give me any sleeping pills."

JoAnn stood up and said, "Try not to worry and I'll be back in a few days. When I return, I'll have something for you. You just be safe in here." "I'm good," Pedro told her.

JoAnn walked out of FDC and placed a call on her cell phone. "Hello," a male voice answered. "My client is fighting, and he's taking his case to trial. There won't be any deals."

"Okay, then we have to get ready for phase two," the man said.

　　After ending the call, JoAnn got inside of her new Cadillac and headed to her next destination. Twenty minutes later, her Cadillac pulled up in front of a privately owned government ran laboratory, on Delaware Avenue. JoAnn was now on a serious mission. She knew it was only a matter of time before the walls would come crumbling down around her.

XXXIX
A FEW HOURS LATER

Queen watched as Sofie walked out of the women's center and got back into the car.

"Is it done," she asked. "Yes it's done," Sofie said, as she reclined back into her seat. Queen started up her car and pulled off down the street.

"How do you feel, be honest with me," Queen asked. Sofie looked over at Queen and said, "I feel sad. I feel like I just killed a part of myself. It's hard to explain, but I feel like a murderer."

Queen pulled her car over to the side of the road and parked. She reached over and grabbed Sofie's hands. "I'm sorry, Babe. I know this is hard for you, but we both know it's something that had to be done. I love you, Sofie, but I love my husband. He is my King, and I'm the only woman who will be the mother of his children. The pregnancy was a mistake. The only way to fix it was getting the abortion. It was what had to be done," Queen said sincerely, "I understand," Sofie replied, but still emotional.

Queen kissed Sofie passionately on the lips and then she pulled off. Queen knew Sofie was hurt, and this was going to be an emotional time for her.

A half-hour later, Queen dropped Sofie off home and drove off. Queen assured Sofie she would call later and check on her. When Sofie entered her home, she fell to her knees in tears. Things were changing. Queen left instead of being her comforter. Sofie understood Queen was married now, but it didn't take away the hurt. She felt empty as she lay on the couch crying out her sorrows.

XL
57th & BALTIMORE AVENUE
SOUTHWEST PHILLY

For two hours, Zeta sat inside of her car watching and waiting. Hours earlier she visited Onyx gentleman's club to ask several questions. After putting together the information she received, she was now on a small block in Southwest Philly. The sky was pitch black and a handful of stars shined above. There was an eerie silence on the block, but that didn't deter Zeta's plans. Tasty's death had been eating her up, and there was nothing anyone could do to help her.

As Zeta sat behind the wheel of her car she watched as the red Volvo parked in front of a two-story home. With a 9mm silencer clutched inside her palm, she exited her vehicle and walked calmly towards the Volvo. Anger begin to set in and revenge pumped in her heart.

When the attractive female got out of her car, Zeta quickly walked up on her. Zeta pushed the gun in the woman's back and instructed her to turn around slowly. As the woman faced Zeta, she shoved the gun into her stomach.

"Your name is Silver," Zeta said. "Yeah, but what's going on," she replied, quivering uncontrollably. "This is for running your mouth and getting my friend, Tasty, murdered."

Zeta squeezed the trigger and shot Silver five times in the stomach. Then she stepped back and watched as Silver fell to the ground, gasping for air. Zeta moved in closer. As Silver tried to call out for help, Zeta unloaded the rest of her bullets into Silver's chest and head.

This was overkill and Zeta would have it no other way. Zeta used the same methods Terry did to get information. Money was all it took for one friend to sing on another in the strip club business. Zeta tossed around some cash and quickly learned that Silver was the woman responsible for giving her girlfriend up to Terry.

Zeta calmly walked over to her running vehicle and got inside. She looked out at Silver's corpse. Silver was a mother of a five-year-old daughter, and now her child would have to deal with the same anguish that Zack felt.

As she pulled off, Zeta whispered to herself, "An eye for an eye. A mother for another." Then she turned on the radio and drove home.

XLI
26TH & RIDGE AVENUE
THEE DAYS LATER

Inside the dimly lit basement of a three-story row home, Vance, Terry, and two of their goons stared at the beaten, bloody man who was tied down to a wooden chair. An hour earlier, they kidnapped the man coming out of an LA Fitness gym on City Line Avenue. The man's face was beaten beyond recognition. He was a mid-level street worker in King's drug organization.

"Nigga I'm gonna ask you one more time! Who killed Carvin and his wife," Vance yelled out. The man refused to talk. Terry then smacked him hard with his .40 caliber pistol.

"So you want to be a tough guy, huh? Terry, kill this son of a bitch," Vance ordered. Terry placed his gun between the man's swollen eyes, but before he pulled the trigger the man said, "It was Biggie! Zeta drove him to Carvin's house!"

"That little bitch ass midget," Vance snapped. "Please, can I go? I gave Y'all what you want," the man begged. "Yeah you can go, motherfucker! You can go whenever God sent Carvin," Terry said, pulling the trigger on his gun and blowing the front of the man's scalp off. "Clean this mess up," Vance told his goons.

Vance and Terry started walking out of the basement, and his cell phone ring. When he noticed who the caller was, he answered quickly.

"What's up Babe? Okay, that's good. I'll see you later tonight," Vance said, ending the call and placing the phone back in his jacket.

With large smiles plastered on their faces, the two men continued to walk out of the basement.

NORTHERN LIBERTIES

After King left the house, Queen, went to get the box her father had given her. She hadn't yet looked at the contents. Queen placed the box on the bed and began to see what was inside.

Inside she found a gold ring, a photo of her mother when she was younger, a silver necklace with a cross, and a small black journal. Queen sat back on the bed and started to read through her mother's diary.

After about forty-five minutes she had read the last sentence. Tears flew down Queen's face after learning about her mother's troubled life as a stripper and a mistress.

As Queen began to place the book into the box, her intuition told her to open it back up. When she looked back at the last page, she realized she hadn't come to the end. There were a few pages skipped and then more writings. Queen took a deep breath and started to read her mother's final words.

It's been so hard dealing with this man. He refuses to give me more. To him, I'm nothing more than a mistress and will never be anything else. Even after giving him a beautiful daughter he still refuses to respect me. And I'm so tired of the verbal abuse and the beatings by his hands. I can't take another black eye or bruised rib.

Lately, I've been feeling so damn sick, and I honestly believe I'm being poisoned. After I found out about his secret meetings with the FBI I've been sick. When I overheard him talking to those two white men, I was utterly shocked to learn that Vance was an informant. He has been working with the FEDS to take down some big time drug dealer named, Face.

How can the man that says he despises snitches become one of them? Life is crazy! Right now I'm just afraid, and I have nowhere to go or hide. All I have left in this world is my beautiful daughter, Queen. I love my baby girl more than life itself, and I hope she always knows that!

Queen was devastated. She had to reread her mother's words two more times to be sure she wasn't dreaming. Tears of anguish and confusion fell down her eyes. She sat on the bed in a daze.

"My father is a snitch! And he poisoned my mother," she shouted out.

Queen thought about the two white men that had been meeting up with her father ever since forever. Now it all made sense. Her mother had discovered her father was an FBI informant, and he poisoned her to keep her quiet.

"So that's why he had her cremated so fast," she thought to herself.

Queen had learned more than she needed to know about her father. For now, she decided to keep this heart-wrenching knowledge to herself. When the time was right, she would confront her dad. But for now, she cried as her hatred for the man who had robbed her from having a mother intensified.

XLII
FEDERAL DETENTION CENTER

Pedro was escorted down a narrow hallway into a private conference room to meet with his lawyer. When he walked inside his attorney was already sitting down waiting for him.

"Sit down. We have to talk," Ms. Morgan said. Pedro sat down and asked, "What's up?" "I notified the Prosecution about your decision to go to trial. They weren't expecting that," Ms. Morgan, seriously told him.

"Fuck them! I don't care what they were expecting! It's about time someone exposes them and all the informants they have working for them," he said. "Did you tell anyone in here about the witness in your case," she asked. "No, because they won't believe me. But, I'm going to show them when Vance's snitch ass gets on the stand." "Good because we don't need anything jeopardizing this important case. Right now the government is afraid. They don't want you to expose one of their key workers," Ms. Morgan said, as she opened up her briefcase and passed Pedro a piece of paper.

"This is what you're being charged with," Ms. Morgan said. Pedro carefully observed the document. "What about the drugs and money," he asked. "What drugs? As far as I know this case has nothing to do with any drugs and the only money retrieved was the twenty-thousand dollars. They stated you were using that to purchase weapons."

Pedro was disgusted. He realized how devious the government agencies were, and how deeply they abused their power.

"Them no good sons of bitches! I paid them two-hundred-twenty-two-thousand dollars for seven kilos of cocaine, and the rest was for weapons. They kept those drugs and all my money except twenty-thousand," Pedro fumed. "Are you sure," she asked. "Yes! I'm sure! They just wanted my money," Pedro yelled.

Twenty minutes later is was time for Pedro to go back to his cell.

"Oh here," Ms. Morgan said, passing Pedro a small brown medicine tube with two pills inside. "Here's the sleeping pills you wanted. Take them right before bed and I'll see you soon. I have some calls to make about your case and that lost money that was confiscated."

After Pedro, left the room Ms. Morgan quickly made a call on her cell phone. "Hello," a male said. "I need to see you. I need to go over some details I just found out about in my client's case," she said. "Okay, you know where I'll be. I'll see you there."

JoAnn Morgan grabbed her briefcase and calmly walked out of the conference room. The severe expression on her face remained, as she drove her car down Arch Street.

43RD STREET
WEST PHILLY

Yellow tape blocked off the entire crime scene from spectators. Police cars and news vans surrounded the area. Standing outside of the yellow tape was King, Biggie, and Zeta. Once again they couldn't believe what they were seeing. Another one of their men had been kidnapped, brutally beaten, murdered and then his naked body was dropped off in the middle of the street.

The words: *King Biggie and Zeta Y'all are next*, was written on his back with a black marker. When the well-paid worker didn't show up for his early morning shift, they knew something was seriously wrong. Rob had been employed with King's organization for two years.

Biggie and Zeta followed King back to his car. The game was claiming bodies left and right, and as strong as they were; they were starting to feel weighed down. The constant looking over their shoulders, the rats, the loss of their worker and family and friends; it was becoming too much.

"We gotta get rid of this nigga, Terry," Zeta said. "I'm tired of feeling like I'm being hunted," she continued. "Yeah, he got to go or else it's gonna continue being an eye for an eye. Ain't no peace while he's still in the game," Biggie replied.

King looked at his two most loyal friends and said, "We have to take off the head! Once the head is gone, then the body will fall," King said gravely. "This guy has been alive for too damn long. We need to find out where he lives or where he hangs out. Killing his workers does nothing because all he does is replace them. We need Vance dead!

I'm still trying to understand why my people on the inside haven't been able to get me the information I need on him. He's like a fuckin ghost. It feels like somebodies protecting him," King said. "Bitch nigga, probably working with the FEDS," Biggie said jokingly. "Don't worry, he can't hide forever. He has to slip up soon," Zeta replied.

"Yeah, that's true. Zeta do you know anything about that stripper who was gunned down outside her home," King said. "Nah, but that was real messed up. Who knows, maybe she finally crossed the wrong person."

King and Biggie watched as Zeta walked away and got back into her car. As she drove off, Biggie said, "You think she did it? "Yeah. She had her reasons," King replied before he and Biggie got inside of his car and drove down the street.

WILLIAM J GREEN JR. FEDERAL BUILDING 6TH & ARCH STREET

Vance's high-powered lawyer, James McDuffie, was having a meeting with the Federal Prosecutor and two FBI Agents.

"Is everything taken care of? My client can't blow his cover, or that'll destroy everything he's done for Y'all." "We are on it counsel. The defendant is stubborn, and he wants to expose your client. If this case goes to trial, then we have no power to keep Vance from taking the stand. We will need him to testify against Mr. Gonzalez to convict him."

James McDuffie stood back shaking his head.

"Don't worry everything will be just fine," one of the agents said confidently. "Yes, Vance will be good, and we will continue to protect our prized asset," the other agent added. James McDuffie and the Federal Prosecutor watched as the two agents smiled and walked out of the office.

"What's that all about," James asked. "I don't know what the FBI is up to counsel. And whatever it is I don't want to know either," the prosecutor told him.

After the meeting had ended, the prosecuting attorney and James went their separate ways. Once James had gotten back into his car he sat in deep thought; concern was written all over his face.

"What the hell is going on that I don't know about," he said to himself. He tried calling Vance, but the call went straight to voicemail.

XLIII
FEDERAL DETENTION CENTER
LATER THAT NIGHT

Pedro struggled to fall asleep as he lay on his top bunk. His troubling thoughts kept him awake, and the discomfort he felt from being in jail didn't help either. Since entering the FDC, sleep was the hardest thing to come by, and the medical staff refused to give him any medication.

All he could think about was Vance setting him up and how he was going to expose him. The thought of it all had been eating him alive for weeks. His trial date was set, and he couldn't wait to see Vance on the witness stand singing and pointing his finger.

After getting on his knees and saying his prayers, Pedro, reached under his pillow and grabbed the two sleeping pills his lawyer had given him. He swallowed them quickly and chased them down with a small bottled water.

As Pedro lay there anticipating the medication's effects, he began to feel strange. His entire body started to tremble uncontrollably, and he couldn't speak as he tried to call out for help. Suddenly a white, foamy substance oozed out of his mouth, as he choked on his saliva.

Pedro's desire to sleep had finally been granted. Less than five minutes after taking those pills he was dead.

BALA CYNWYD, PA

Vance watched as the beautiful, naked woman walked over and joined him in his bed. "Thanks, Babe, for everything," he said, as he began kissing her soft, full breast. "Anything for you, Love," JoAnn responded. "Pedro should be nice and dead by now. I'm sure he took those cyanide pills that your friends gave me. The way he was complaining about sleeping, I'm sure he's out like a light now. So all your worries are gone," she continued. Vance slid down between JoAnn's legs and started eating her pussy.

For over three years Vance and JoAnn Morgan had been having a secret affair. The only people who knew about them were the two FBI agents Vance had been working for.

Outside of the Agents and JoAnn, no one knew about their secret plot to kill Pedro. Once word came back that Pedro was going to trial, he had signed his own death warrant. The plan had been in motion for weeks. Vance was a major asset for the FEDS, and they had no intentions of letting him be exposed. There were no limits they wouldn't go to keep his identity a secret and Pedro had to learn that lesson the hard way.

XLIV
EARLY THE NEXT MORNING

The Federal Detention Center was on lockdown. A Correctional Officer discovered Pedro lifeless body on his bunk when he didn't get up for count time. Pedro's untimely and suspicious death had authorities in a panic. A staff investigation had taken place, and the FBI had joined in. All inmates were locked in their cells with no access to the phones.

Pedro's death was plastered on the front page of the Philadelphia Daily Newspaper. His entire neighborhood was in mourning. Pedro had been a legend and a standup man in his hood. Now their legend was dead and gone, and presently no one had answers as to why.

NORTHEAST PHILLY

"I got some real good info on Vance's whereabouts," Plex, said to Bobby. "From who," Bobby questioned. "A good source," Plex snapped. "Okay then let's see what's up," Bobby said, as he pulled off down the street.

"Not yet. When the time is right, I'm on Vance and Terry's ass. First I have to make sure the info is right. I don't want to kill another innocent man. I need Vance and Terry to get what's meant for them, and them only," Plex said, finally sounding as if he had some sense.

Bobby pulled into a Checkers' fast food drive through and ordered. After they had gotten their food, he pulled off down the Boulevard.

NORTHERN LIBERTIES

King noticed the change in Queen's attitude and demeanor. He watched as she sat on the sofa, consumed with her thoughts, and then he walked over to her.

"What's wrong? You've been a little distant lately. Did I do something wrong," King asked. Queen reached out and grabbed King's hands. "No Love, you're fine. I've just had a lot on my mind, but I'm good."

King smiled, but he could plainly see something was bothering Queen. She hardly ate and wasn't sleeping throughout the night.

"Whenever you're ready to talk I'm here for you," King said, as he sat down beside her. King firmly placed his arms around her body and kissed Queen gently on the cheek.

"I love you, Queen." "I love you too, Hun! Please don't be worried about me, I'm okay. I just need some sleep so I can empty my mind," Queen replied.

"Okay, is everything cool with you and Sofie," King asked. "We good. That's not it. It's something else but I'll that care of it when the time is right. Trust me. You and I are good, Babe."

XLV
UPPER DARBY, PA

Vance looked at all the people who were seated at the round table. He had called a meeting for all the bosses in Philly to attend. Inside the meeting was Russian Mobster Victor Gavrikov, Chinese Triad Kingpin Billy Chan, Colombian Queenpin Rosa Gomez, and Italian mobster Tommy Marino. His right-hand man Terry and a few of his street lieutenants also sat at the table.

"I called this meeting with hopes we can bring our crews together and take over this entire city. For years, we have been warring and fighting over the same money. If we unite our organizations, we could be unstoppable! Billy, you have the largest shipments of heroin coming in. Victor, you have all the guns. Rosa, you have the coke and weed, and Tommy has all the pills that enter the city limits. If we combine forces, this town will be ours!"

Billy Chan stood up from the table. He was a short guy, standing around 5 foot 4.

"What about King? He is the biggest cocaine dealer in Philly. How can we take over without him," Billy Chan asked. "Fuck King! His reign is coming to an end. And I heard some terrible things about King," Vance said. "What's that," Tommy Marino asked.

Vance looked around the table and said, "I heard that King's an informant. He's working with the FEDS." "Nah, not King. I used to deal with his cousin Face, and he's a standup guy," Tommy responded. "I'm telling you what I heard from a good source," Vance said.

"I heard King was a good dude too but fuck him, I'm rolling with you Vance," Rosa added. "I'm with you too! If King is a snitch he should die," Victor said.

Vance looked over at Billy and asked, "What do you think? " "I like the idea of joining our organizations, but it's hard for me to believe that King is an informant. His cousin is a legend and King's name has been good on the streets since he took over."

Vance became frustrated with Tommy and Billy. He knew both men had worked with Face before King had taken over, and he could see they still had an alliance with Face's dynasty.

After the meeting had ended, Vance stood back and watched as Tommy and Bill got into their cars and drove away.

"What do you think about them two," Victor asked? "If they are not with us, they are against us," Vance answered. "Well fuck them too! I can't stand wops and Chinks anyway," Rosa replied. "I'm with you, Vance. Whatever you need I'm here. Fuck King's snitch ass," Rosa continued. Vance kissed Rosa on the cheek and said, "I'll be calling you soon. Be safe."

Rosa walked to her Mercedes and got inside. When she pulled off, Vance stood with Terry and Victor.

"Are we still going to the fight on Saturday," Terry asked. "Yeah, you wanna come with us, Victor," Vance asked. "No, I'm not a big fight fan. Plus I have other business to take care of," Victor said, winking his eye.

Vance smiled and said, "Just do it quick and quiet."
"Don't worry my friend, that's the only way us Russians do it," he said, as they all laughed.

CHESTER, PA

King and Biggie watched as the workers carried large duffel bags of cocaine into the warehouse. A shipment of twenty-five-hundred kilos had just been dropped off. Zeta observed the workers carefully as she held her loaded 9mm to her side. She didn't trust anyone. King's cell phone rang.

"What's up Billy, long time no hear from," King said. "Yes, I've been busy getting the money. Like you," Billy replied. "But I'm calling you now to warn you about something," he continued. "What's that," King asked. "You need to watch out for that dude, Vance. He's plotting on you heavy. He's trying to take you down. I just left a meeting with him, the Russian, Rosa and Tommy. This guy is attempting to take over the whole city, and he's teaming up with all the other bosses."

"So you and Tommy fucking with Vance now," King snapped. "Naw, Homie. Me and Tommy both rolled out. We wasn't feeling him at all. Plus we stay loyal to the ones who've been around since day one. We don't go back on our words," Billy promised.

"That's what's up, Billy," King replied. "Oh and that's not all," Billy said. "In the meeting, Vance told everyone that you're an informant who's working for the FEDS," he continued. "What," King fumed. "Yeah, but me and Tommy knew that was a lie, so we rolled out. This guy is trying to ruin your good name, and he got Victor and Rosa believing him."

King couldn't believe Vance would stoop so low. King would never rat. However, Vance would say anything out his mouth to crush King's empire.

"So where did yall meet up," King asked. "I'll text you the location when I get home. Just be safe out here, and you need to handle your business. This problem won't just go away, and I think you know what you have to do. It's about to be crazy, and it's going to come down to you or him. I think you know what I'm saying," Billy said. "I'm on it, Billy. Thanks again for the heads up," King said. "Anytime, and tell my man Face I said hello."

King spoke to Biggie and Zeta about the call from Billy Chan. After the drug shipment was handled, they got back into their cars and headed towards Southwest Philly. The game plan was in effect, and their next move was to eliminate the head before he had their necks.

GERMANTOWN

When Queen walked into Sofie's apartment, she was sitting on the couch crying. Queen walked over to her friend and sat beside her.

"What's wrong?" Sofie looked into Queen's caring eyes and said, "I'm lonely. I've been lonely ever since you married King. We don't spend any time together, and we hardly talk anymore. I feel so alone."

Queen put her arms around Sofie's shoulders and said, "I am married now Sofie, but you know I'll always be here for you. We have an unbreakable bond, and I'm busier than I've been before, but if you need me, I'll be here. I won't lie to you. My husband comes first, but we will always be friends."

"I understand you, Queen, but why have you been ignoring me? I had to call and text you over ten times just to get you here," Sofie cried out. "It's nothing personal, Sofie. Sometimes you call when I'm in bed with King and I can't just get up and leave, or be on the phone. Like I said, it's nothing personal just a part of married life."

Queen stood up to leave and said, "I'm going to call you later. I have a doctor's appointment, and I can't miss it."

Sofie watched Queen walk out the door. She was fuming with anger. Sofie had just told her friend that she needed her, that she felt alone, and again she brushed her off. She cried, but her tears quickly turned into rage. How could Queen just discard of her as if she was nothing more than a typical girlfriend? The two had been through too much, and Sofie did not like being tossed aside like a piece of garbage.

XLVI
LATER THAT NIGHT
BALA, CYNWYD

JoAnn's deep moans filled the air inside of the bedroom. Tonight Vance had taken a Viagra pill to extend his sexual performance. It had already been two hours, and Vance had fucked JoAnn's body in every way imaginable. With each stroke from Vance's hard dick, JoAnn came uncontrollably.

Vance turned JoAnn onto her stomach, and spread her legs apart, before climbing on top of her naked physique. Swiftly, Vance slid his dick inside her ass. JoAnn tried to brace herself, but his hard dick went full force. And once inside of her ass she exploded. She was lost in a world of pure bliss. Orgasms swept throughout her quivering body.

Vance controlled her body like no other man had ever done before. And for giving her body what it needed, she'd do anything Vance asked without any hesitancy.

NORTHERN LIBERTIES

"Don't open your eyes yet," Queen said, as she walked King into the bedroom. "What's this surprise," he asked. "You will find out soon! Just keep your eyes closed."

Queen, walked King, over to the bed and sat him down. Then she reached under the pillow and placed a small card on his lap.

"Okay, now you can open your eyes," Queen said to him. "What's this," he asked. "Just open it up and read it."

King opened the card and started reading the message.

I love you more than any words I could ever say. You are everything that I ever wanted in a man. No matter what life brings our way, I will be by your side to the very end.

Love always — The mother of your CHILD.

When King read the last word, he looked up at Queen as she stood in front of him holding a positive pregnancy test.

"I'm pregnant baby! I'm early, no more than six weeks, but we're going to have a baby," she said tearfully. King stood up and hugged her tightly. "When did you find out," he asked. "Today at my doctor's appointment." King was excited beyond words. He couldn't think of another woman who was fit to bear his child than his Queen.

For a few silent moments, they held each. Tears of joy continued to flow from Queen's eyes.

"If it's a girl I want to name her Sianni," King said. "Well, it's not going to be a girl. I can feel a handsome little boy growing inside me," Queen said, smiling. She continued, "It will be a boy, and his name will be Prince; the son of King and Queen."

XLVII
10:10 P.M.
CHINATOWN

Victor Gavrikov watched from his tinted, black truck, as a small group of Asian men walked into the Ring Wong Restaurant. For two hours he had stalked the spot, waiting for the perfect opportunity to strike. Sitting beside him was his younger sister, Natasha. She was an attractive, tall brunette with piercing green eyes.

When it was the time, they exited the vehicle and walked across the street into the crowded restaurant. A waiter escorted them to an empty table in the back. As soon as they were seated, Natasha went inside of her large pocketbook and passed Victor the loaded Tech-9, a gas mask, and a smoke bomb. In her hand, she gripped a Glock 17 and a smoke bomb in the other.

Natasha stood up and walked to the front of the restaurant. The place was so busy that no one paid her any attention. Suddenly, Natasha, dropped the smoke bomb on the floor and instantly a cloud of smoke appeared. In the back of the restaurant, Victor had dropped his smoke bomb, causing the same hazy effect. The restaurant was now filled with smoke that was coming from all directions.

Before dropping the smoke bombs, Victor and Natasha had located their targets. Now with his gas mask on, Victor, walked over to Billy Chan's table.

Pow! Pow! Pow! Pow! Pow! Pow! Pow!

Victor shot Billy Chan three times in the head, and everyone at his table was mortally wounded. The crowd was in

complete chaos. People screamed and rushed the entrance door. Natasha stood guard, shooting anyone who tried to exit. The screaming and terrified customers were falling like flies caught in a Venus Flytrap.

When the thick smoke started to fade, Victor and Natasha had eased out of the restaurant; leaving a trail of bullet-ridden bodies behind them. In total, fifteen people had lost their lives tonight.

Victor pulled off down the street and looked at his sister and said, "Good job Natasha." Victor then turned his truck on 9th Street as he headed over to South Philly. "Thanks, big brother. Anything for you and the organization," Natasha said, as she set back and reloaded their weapons.

GERMANTOWN

Sofie placed the loaded .38 inside of her mouth for the fourth time. However, each time she was afraid to pull the trigger. Lately, she had been feeling so alone. Suicidal thoughts roamed through her mind.

Sofie stood up from the sofa and paced back and forth inside of the living room. There was a wall of hatred inside of her that was built off of King's image. King was the one who had taken the one person who mattered most. He was the reason she was in this dark space feeling empty.

Sofie looked over at the bottle of sleeping pills that were on the coffee table. She walked over and picked up the bottle of pills. She stared at the bottle, but once again her fears kept her from opening the bottle up. Sofie dropped the bottle of pills to the floor and rushed to the sofa. There she cried as she held a gun on her lap. "Why can't I just end it," she cried out.

XLVIII
UPPER DARBY, PA

Biggie had the infrared beam on his target's forehead. Before the man could recognize he was being hunted, Biggie pulled the trigger and blew a quarter sized hole in his head.

"Good shot! Now let's burn this fucking place down," Zeta said, as she and Biggie walked from behind a row of trees. After Billy Chan had given King the address to Vance's meeting spot, he passed the information on to his two top hitters, Biggie, and Zeta.

Holding a container of gasoline in her hands, Zeta, walked past the carcasses as Biggie followed behind. Located on the outskirts of Philly, the small warehouse was one of Vance's meeting and stash spots. Inside were several boxes of marijuana, stacked up wall high. Zeta quickly walked around the warehouse pouring gasoline while Biggie stood by the door keeping watch.

After emptying the gas out, she lit a match and watched as the flames instantly lit up the warehouse. Zeta and Biggie rushed out and returned to their car.

"Yeah, fuck them, niggas," Biggie shouted out like an excited child. Zeta pulled off down the secluded road. When Zeta looked in the rearview mirror, all she could see was an enormous cloud of smoke and flames coming from the burning warehouse.

"Yeah, fuck them, niggas," Zeta said, as they celebrated their victory.

XLIX
SOUTH PHILLY

The outside of Geno's Steaks was crowded with an endless line of people. Geno's was one of the most famous cheesesteak restaurants in town. Tommy Marino and two of his men were standing around talking. They never noticed the beautiful, tall blonde who was standing just a few feet behind them.

From a distance, Victor watched as his sister inched closer. As Tommy, and his friend continued to talk, Natasha had her hand inside her purse clutching a loaded .40 caliber with an attached silencer. She eased through the boisterous crowd as she approached her unsuspecting target. POW! POW! POW! POW! POW! POW!

Tommy and his two henchmen fell to the ground. Natasha then stood over Tommy's body and fired two more rounds into his chest. The scene was chaotic as bystanders and employees rushed for cover. When Natasha was satisfied that her target was dead, she walked away.

"Good job Sis," Victor said, as he watched Natasha take off her blonde wig. Natasha looked over at her brother and smiled before they sped away.

BALA CYNWYD, PA

Vance lay on his back with his eyes closed as JoAnn pleasingly performed oral sex. She slid her wet, warm mouth up and down his rock hard dick and he was in heaven. When his cell phone rang, he tried to ignore it, but the constant ringing meant someone needed his immediate attention.

"Wassup, Vic," Vance said, heavily because JoAnn was still all over his dick. "Tommy and Billy are on a permanent vacation, Boss. You will read about them in the morning papers," Victor said, with an evil laugh. "Good, I kneew...I could count on you," Vance said, as he placed his right hand on top of JoAnn's head as she swallowed him whole. After hanging up the phone, Vance burst his thick, warm nut into JoAnn's yearning mouth.

Afterward, Vance sat up and thought about the great news he had received. Victor and Natasha were his secret weapons. They were loyal and would off anyone who crossed him. Vance knew while he was in this war he had to keep those two close. They were a necessity he couldn't afford to lose.

L
EARLY THE NEXT MORNING

When Vance learned his worker had been murdered, and the half-ton of marijuana and his warehouse were burned down, he was livid. He quickly called Victor and Terry and demanded they add extra security on all his stash spots and drug locations.

The war with King wasn't going as easy as he thought it would. King and his crew had turned out to be a burden and thorn in his side. As JoAnn lay sleeping beside him, Vance was in deep thought. All he could think about was the many ways he wanted to torture and kill King. The only way he could feel any peace was to have King's head on a silver platter.

RITTENHOUSE SQUARE

King couldn't believe the terrible news he had just received from Biggie. Tommy Marino and Billy Chan had been viciously executed. Everyone on the streets was talking about it. They were two well-known bosses, and their deaths sent a clear message that there was a war. King knew Vance was the culprit behind the savage slayings.

"Are you okay, Babe," Queen asked, as she sat beside him on the sofa. "Not really, but I will be once I get this thorn out my side," King replied. "Who is the thorn? For the last few weeks something or someone has been irritating you," she said. "It's all good. I'm going to fix this problem real soon. I don't want to stress you out right now with my personal issues. This is my business, and I'll take care of it.

You just take care of my little prince." King said. "Okay Love, but if you ever want to talk, I'm right here," Queen said.

King kissed Queen and stood up from the sofa.

"What's your plans for the day," King asked. "Nothing much. I need to get something to eat. It's too early for these cravings, and they keep changing up on me. Yesterday it was pickles, today its butter pecan ice-cream. I'll probably visit my girlfriend too after I satisfy my cravings."

"Okay, call me if you need me. I love you," King said as he walked away. Queen walked over to the window and watched as King got into his Mercedes and drove off. She had to handle some serious business of her own.

LI
56TH & MARKET
WEST PHILLY

"I can't stand a Rat! There is nothing on this earth worse than a snitch and an undercover faggot," Biggie shouted.

Zeta and Haze loaded their guns with Teflon bullets while Biggie vented out his anger towards informants.

"Snitches took down John Gotti, Big Meech, Freeway Rick Ross, Wayne Perry, Guy Fisher, and Aaron Jones from JBM, and so many other good men. What the hell happened to the code of the streets! What happened to death before dishonor! These new wannabe drug dealers and gangstas are fucking the game up! They all need to die, so we can bring back them real niggas from the 70's, 80's, and early 90's! "

"Shit changed, man. The FEDS got all these new niggas snitching for less time. I heard Lil Junie snitched on his own grandma to get less time. And she got locked up with his drugs," Haze said, shaking his head. "Yeah, that was fucked up. Now he back out on the streets while his grandma doing a thirty-six-month bid somewhere in West Virginia," Zeta said. "You serious," Biggie asked. "I didn't know Junie ratted on his peeps."

"Yup, it's true! Everybody knows what Junie did was some foul shit. Check this shit out," Haze said, pulling out a laptop computer. "This is the Federal Inmate Locator website. I'm gonna type in Junie grandma and show you something."

Biggie and Zeta were in total amazement when they saw a photo of Junie's grandma. Her release date and charges also appeared on the screen.

"See, I told you, man! Junie snitched on his own grandma," Haze said, as he sat back shaking his head in disgust. "What nigga snitches on his own grandmother," Zeta asked. Biggie looked at Zeta and Haze. They could see the hatred and anger that had instantly filled his eyes.

"A dead one," Biggie said before he tucked his loaded 9mm under his shirt and walked out the door.

"I don't know why you got him started Haze. You know how Biggie feels about Rats," Zeta said, as she raced out after him.

LII
CAMDEN, NJ

Rosa Gomez was a boss in every sense of the word. She was the leader of her own cartel, comprised of violent Colombian drug dealers and killers. She also had major connects with the Dominican and Puerto Rican mob. There were rumors that Rosa was the great niece of former drug kingpin Pablo Escobar, of the Medellin cartel. Her crew was responsible for over three hundred murders up and down the East coast. Rosa ruled her empire with murder and torture. Anyone who had crossed her never lived to talk about it.

Rosa walked down into the basement, surrounded by four of her most loyal soldiers. Strapped onto a long wooden table was a naked Latin man. He had been brutally beaten, and he clung to life. Rosa walked over to the beaten man and lifted his head so he could see her eyes.

"Where is my cocaine, Carlos? This is your last chance to save yourself, so speak up" she demanded. "I...I...told you I was robbed Rosa! I don't know who it was, but they robbed me. They had on a black mask," Carlos said, as blood dripped from his mouth.

"Okay, then. Since you want to stick to that same story, I have no choice but to do what I'm about to do! You fuck me, and I fuck you harder," Rosa said, as she walked to a shelf and grabbed a metal pipe. With the pipe clutched in her right hand, Rosa walked behind Carlos. She ordered two of her men to spread his legs wider.

"Please, Rosa! Please! Nooooooooo!!!" Rosa ignored Carlo's cries as she continued to shove the metal pipe far up his anus.

"Aahhhhh! Ahhhh!!!" Carlos's screams filled the room. The pain he was suffering was unbearable. Rosa pushed the pipe up as far as it would go. Each time she pulled the pipe out it was covered with blood and muscle tissue. Rosa was literally fucking Carlos to death, and she enjoyed it. She loved to humiliate anyone who crossed her.

When Carlos' screams had faded, and he could no longer speak, Rosa pulled out her .380 and shot him twice in the head.

LIII
DOWNTOWN PHILADELPHIA

The Loews Hotel is one of the most inviting, luxurious hotels in Philadelphia. It's located along the bustling Market Street, in the city's oldest skyscrapers. Inside one of its luxurious rooms, Vance and two FBI agents were seated having a discussion.

"There's another shipment of cocaine and heroin coming in next week from your girl Rosa, over in Jersey. We learned about that some time ago. We're going to need your men to do what they did before," Agent Toney said. Vance sat calmly and replied, "No problem. I will have it done, and once it's sold, you'll get your money like always."

Agent Lucas walked over to Vance and said, "Do you think anyone knows you've been cooperating with the FBI?" "No, nobody knows. The only person who knew was found dead in his prison cell," Vance said, as they started laughing.

"You have been robbing major drug dealers for almost twenty years. Are you ready to call it quits," Agent Toney asked? Vance looked sternly at the two agents. "Hell no! I'm a multi-millionaire because of what I do. Why would I want to stop getting money and let go of my get-out-of-jail-free card?"

"What about the code of the streets everyone talks about," Agent Lucas asked. "Fuck that code," Vance replied. "Working with the FEDS has made me untouchable! I'm gonna die when you two retire on me," he said.

"Wassup with that nigga King," Vance asked. "We are still looking, but he's been covering his tracks well. We believe he has different locations all over the city. It's hard to track him down like the others. Besides, no one in his crew is talking. That makes his circle hard to penetrate," Agent Lucas said. "He learned a thing or two from his cousin, Face; I'm sure," Agent Toney replied.

Vance stood up and said, "Fuck King, and his cousin Face! King is going down, and sooner or later his bitch ass is mine." Agent Lucas looked over at his partner and then turned to Vance.

"Calm down, Vance. You've given us what we need, and I'm sure you'll get what you want. We're headed back to the office, but you can trust that we are working on it. We'll be in touch," Agent Lucas said, as he and his partner left the hotel room.

LIV
30TH STREET TRAIN STATION

The yellow cab pulled up in front of the train station and double parked. After paying the old gray haired cabbie, Sofie got out of the cab carrying a small suitcase. She wanted to get away. Somewhere, anywhere, would do. The past few weeks Sofie and Queen had been the most distant they'd ever been. The separation was slowly killing Sofie on the inside.

Sofie walked through the crowded train terminal and found an empty bench. She sat down as she watched people coming and going. Her mind was clouded. There were thoughts filled with anger, betrayal, but her heart longed to be close to Queen again. Sofie realized suicide wasn't the answer, but she didn't know what to do to overcome her agony.

As she sat down in anguish, all she could do was cry. She was deeply depressed. Her eyes were bloodshot red from non-stop crying. She looked over at the ticket box office. After debating within herself if she should stay or go, Sofie stood up from the bench and grabbed her suitcase. She walked out of the train station and moments later was in the back of a cab headed home.

"If I hurt, then so will she," Sofie murmured, as her tears continued to fall from her eyes.

WAYNE & CHELTEN AVENUE

Biggie and Zeta were inside of a car that was parked across the street from Wendy's fast food restaurant. They were watching the cars drive as they drove in and out of the drive through. Zeta looked over at Biggie and saw nothing but hatred in his eyes.

Zeta and Biggie had a strong bond. It didn't matter what Biggie asked her to do; she could never tell him no. She looked at him as a brother, and she pledged always to have his back. Biggie would give his life for Zeta, and their connection was one that could never be broken.

When the traffic slowed down at Wendy's, Biggie, looked over at Zeta, and said, "You ready?" She replied, "Yeah, I'm ready Homie," before starting up the car and slowly pulling off.

Zeta drove the car into Wendy's parking lot and pulled beside two parked cars. While Zeta waited, Biggie sat holding the .40 caliber. Zeta then drove the car in the drive-through line. There were two cars ahead of her.

As the cars before her got their orders, Biggie inconspicuously got into the backseat. Zeta moved the car to the driveway window, and Biggie crept out of the back door and blended in with the wall. He had on his black mask, hiding his face. When the sliding glass window opened, a man stuck his head out and said, "Hi, can I help you?"

Zeta smiled and placed a bogus order as Biggie crept up. "Large fries, chicken nuggets and a Vanilla milkshake." The man smiled at the beautiful woman and said, "Okay, that will be twelve dollars and eighteen cents, but it's on the house if you let me call you."

The man watched as Zeta dug into her purse for the money and ignored his request. Suddenly, Biggie appeared with his gun aimed at the guy's head.

"Yo Junie, this for snitching on your grandma!" Biggie squeezed the trigger and unloaded his weapon, sending multiple bullets into Junie's skull and body.

His co-workers begin screaming and running for cover. They were terrified at the sight of the gruesome scene. Biggie quickly jumped into the backseat of the car and Zeta peeled off. Biggie had completed another one of his personal missions; killing another Rat.

BALA CYNWYD, PA

"Are we still going to the Hopkins fight," Terry asked. "Yeah, we still good to go," Vance replied, as they sat back counting a large stack of money which was laid out on the table. Terry had the utmost respect for his boss. He looked up to him and loved his diehard, street, demeanor. In his eyes, Vance was a true gangster and drug dealer.

As Terry sat back counting the money, he listened as Vance vented out his hatred for King, Face, and snitches. All the while he had no clue that he was in the presence of the ultimate Rat.

LV
TWO DAYS LATER
PORTA HELI, GREECE

Ranked as one of the top ten, most exotic places in the world Porto Heli, Greece was visually striking. The region housed lush olive groves to perfect bays. Every scene seemed as if it was lifted from a postcard.

Walking down the private beach resort Face and Quincy talked about the current state of the Philly Underworld. For months, it had been in complete chaos. Though Face and his family were on vacation, traveling around the world, he still kept his ears on the scene.

"What's going on now," Face asked Quincy. "Same shit! It's fucked up in Philly, but King is handling his business and living up to the Smith name. He just needs to hit his target and bring down that murder rate. The more bodies they have on the streets, the more heat he'll have on him," Quincy replied. "King knows the game. He knows exactly what he needs to do," Face said. "Man, you sure you don't want to step in and help him before shit gets even more fucked up," his right-hand said. "We can't Q! Not this time. King has to do it himself. With his crew and no interference from us. We are retired. We lost Reece, Veronica, and so many others we loved and cared for. The torch has been passed to the next generation of hustlers. I love my Lil cousin, but I can't fight his battles for him. I fought all mine and from where I stand, we won. King must do the same," Face explained.

"You're right. We did our job. We made it out of that heartless game alive and now King has to lay his own road," Quincy said, in agreement with Face.

...

"Damn! Where'd you get that info from," Bobby asked Plex as he looked at the piece of paper. "Don't worry, just know that nigga can't hide forever," Plex said. "Niggas gonna pay for what they did to my wife!"

Bobby started up his car and drove out of his apartment building's parking lot. As Plex vented out his anger, Bobby quickly made his way to Southwest Philly.

LVI
7TH & SNYDER
SOUTH PHILLY

Inside a tinted black Lincoln MKT, Johnnie Marino and Chow-men Chan were having a secret meeting. They were the older brothers of, Billy Chan and Tommy Marino, who had been savagely gunned down just a few days earlier. Because of the untimely deaths of their brothers, these two men had inherited their drug organizations.

"We have to kill the motherfuckers responsible for the deaths of our brothers," Johnnie said. Chow-men Chan just sat there nodding his head in agreement. He was a quiet but very dangerous man. Many people agreed he was the most ruthless of the Chan brothers.

"I'm hearing that Vance or King had something to do with their murders," Johnnie said. Once again Chow just nodded his head in agreement. "They both went to a meeting with Vance, and afterward, they are each assassinated. So either Vance had it done because he didn't like something they did or said, or King had them murdered because he felt betrayed," Johnnie said. "I say we put out hits on both of them," he continued.

Chow took off his glasses and looked Johnnie square in the eyes. "An innocent man should never die because of another man's actions," Chow said. "We find out the true culprit and that person die. We will meet again in a few days," Chow said. The new bosses shook hands and departed.

Today, Chow and Johnnie had decided to join forces to find out who was responsible for killing their brothers. Neither man would rest until someone had paid for their sins. They knew they needed to make a move soon because whoever had killed their brothers, would certainly have no problem coming for their heads. The countdown had begun.

LVII
RITTENHOUSE SQUARE
SOUTH PHILLY

"Are you sure you want me to go to your father's house with you," King asked. "Yes, I'm sure. I want you to wait in the car first because I have something very important to talk to him about," Queen replied. "Sure, but is everything okay? You're still distant. What's up with Sofie? Did you get in contact with her yet," King asked, as he sat down beside Queen and held her.

"Everything is fine. I just have to have a serious talk with my father. Sofie hasn't been answering my phone calls. She's upset with me because I'm taking a break from her, but she'll get over it," Queen replied. "What time will you be ready," Queen asked. "A little later tonight." "Okay cool, I have a few runs to make, but I'll be back by seven," King said.

After kissing Queen on her soft, plump lips, King stood up and walked over to the door. "Call your friend and see what's up with her. That girl loves you, and sometimes people can't handle rejection. People do stupid or crazy shit when they're in pain. So call her," King said, as he walked out the front door.

Queen reached over and grabbed her cell phone from off the table. She called Sofie, and it went straight to voicemail. After calling two more times and still getting no answer, Queen gave up. She then reached under the sofa and pulled out her mother's journal. In the silence of the living room, Queen sat on the couch, letting the tears fall from her eyes as she thought of her mother's memories.

GERMANTOWN

Sofie sat on the bed watching as the calls came in from Queen. Initially, she pushed the first call to voicemail, but then she let her phone rang until it went to voicemail automatically.

She had no interest in talking to her former friend and lover, Queen. In her heart and soul, she had been betrayed. As she lay in bed crying, beside her was the Holy Bible and a loaded .38 pistol. Her eyes were red and stained with blood. The pain inside of her was incurable. She was lost in her world of chaos, lust and love. And she now blamed it all on Queen.

LVIII
29TH & ALLEGHENY AVENUE

King sat at the head of a long table with his crew members seated around him. Inside the room was his bodyguard Nas, Haze, Zark, Zeta, and Biggie.

"We have to be on point more than before when we're out on these streets. I hear Vance is responsible for killing Billy and Tommy. He has some Russian hit-man on his payroll and some cops. They are all out to bring us down. I'm sure the FEDS are on us as well."

King stood up and looked at everyone's faces.
"I don't want to lose another person in my crew. Zark is back, and we almost lost him. We have to be smarter than everyone else out here! Shit is getting hectic, and if we plan to stay the top dogs in Philly we need to be fifty steps ahead of everyone out here," King shouted.

"I agree," Biggie said, and everyone else nodded their heads in agreement. "I want yall to move out of your current spots and relocate. Everyone has to change their phones and even switch up your cars. Remember, only use your personal info if you have to, and you don't have to. We have to switch up our routines, so we don't get too comfortable or predictable. Predictability gets you killed," King reminded them.

After the brief meeting, everyone went their separate ways. Biggie, Zark, and Haze planned to go to the Bernard Hopkins fight in a few hours while Zeta went to take care of some personal business. King and his bodyguard were headed to another meeting.

60TH & LANSDOWNE AVENUE
WEST PHILLY

"It's on tonight, Homie! Niggas is gonna feel all my pain," Plex said, as he set back loading a Remington 700 sniper rifle with a scope attached. Bobby sat next to him listening. Plex was filled with excitement.

"Niggas killed my wife! Now it's payback! They got me all the way fucked up," Plex shouted.

After loading the rifle Plex stood up and walked over to the wall mantle. It housed pictures and antiques. Plex held a photo with him and his wife in it and wept.

"Don't worry baby girl, they're all gonna pay for what they did to you."

LIX
ROOSEVELT BOULEVARD
NORTHEAST PHILLY

The Black Range Rover pulled up and parked in the back of the IHOP restaurant. Vance and Terry stepped out and walked over to a waiting Mercedes Benz minivan. When they got in, Victor and Natasha were inside waiting for them.

"I need another job done tonight," Vance said. "Sure. Just give us all the details and it will be done," Victor replied. Vance passed Victor a small piece of paper and said, "Everything you need to know is on there. Get rid of it when you're done." "No problem Bossman. I'll call you later when the job is done," Victor said. Then he and his sister watched as Vance and Terry exited their car and pulled off in theirs.

"We have a big job to do later tonight, are you ready," Victor asked. "I'm always ready," Natasha replied before she started up the van and pulled off.

Thirty minutes later, Victor and Natasha arrived at a small apartment near Bridge & Pratt. They walked into the back room and opened a closet. Inside the closet was a treasure trove of weapons, ammunition, bulletproof vests, gas masks, hand grenades and knives. There was enough artillery to supply a small Army.

After loading all the weapons they would need for their next assignment into the van, Natasha and Victor drove towards New Jersey.

WEST RIVER DRIVE

Zeta parked her car. Then she walked around the car to open up the passenger door for her godson, Zack. When she looked into his eyes, she couldn't help but cry.

"Are you okay Auntie Z," he asked. Zeta grabbed his small hand and said, "Yes, I just miss your mother so much."

They started walking down the park's pathway, and Zack paused and said, "My mommy is in heaven. One day we will get to see her again. God promised us." Zeta smiled and said, "Yup, we sure will."

Zeta fought back her tears as she and Zach walked down the pathway. She had about an hour to spend with him before she had to get to her next destinations. Zeta did her best to dry up her eyes and enjoy their limited time.

LX
BROAD STREET

The Liacouras Center was one of Philly's largest venues for sports and cultural events. Situated in the heart of North Philadelphia. Tonight the biggest event in the city was being held under its roof. Middleweight champion and Philly native Bernard "B-Hop" Hopkins was defending his World Boxing Council (WBC) belt.

The energetic crowd filled the venue to capacity. Celebrities, musicians, hustlers, gangstas and Divas lined the seats. The excited eyes from all spectators were focused on the massive twenty-five-foot ring that was located in the middle of the arena.

Vance and Terry had front row seats. A few seats down from them, we're some of Philly's most respected and successful celebrities. Meek Mill, Will Smith, Charlie Mack, Eve, Jimmy DaSaint, Bradley Cooper, Danny Garcia, Allen Iverson, Patty LaBelle and many more.

Vance sat in his seat like a boss. He looked at all the people around him, and he wasn't impressed with any of the so-called celebrities. Vance didn't admire anyone, no matter who they were and what they did. He very often had the tendency to look down on everyone. For twenty years he had been a successful drug dealer, with the FBI supporting his every move, he was making million, and he felt untouchable.

Just a few rows back Biggie, Haze, and Zark, were watching one of the preliminary fights. The main event was still a few bouts away. As Biggie observed the crowd he noticed a familiar face. Vance and Terry were sitting beside one another, and Biggie couldn't believe his eyes. He thought about going down to them and killing them on the spot. However, he knew he wouldn't make it out of the venue without being caught. The place was jam-packed with Philadelphia Police Officers.

Biggie took this moment to plan as he kept his eyes on his targets. When the fight was over, he was going to kill Vance and Terry while they walked to their cars.

He took out his cellphone and text Zeta:
Need you at the fight. I got both our enemies!

LXI
CAMDEN, NEW JERSEY

Known as the most violent city in America, Camden, New Jersey was right across the bridge from Philadelphia. Murders, kidnappings, guns and drugs filled Camden's streets. The murder rate was so severe that state officials placed a nine o' clock curfew on all its citizens.

On the corner of Sheridan Street, Victor and Natasha finally spotted the large U-Haul truck. Only a few people knew what contents were inside the van, and Victor and Natasha were two of them.

Parked inside a tinted black Ford Taurus, Victor had his FR-F2 sniper rifle fixed on his target. A silencer was attached to muffle the sound. It also had an infrared telescope to guarantee him a perfect shot. Before coming to America, Victor was a former member of the Russian KGB. He was highly skilled in covert missions, espionage, hand to hand battles, and assassinations.

The sky was dark and filled with several stars and a full moon. Victor sat as still as he could. When the U-Haul stopped at the corner, Victor had the driver's head in his crosshairs. With one pull of the trigger, Victor watched as the driver slumped back in his seat. Pieces of brain matter and flesh covered the steering wheel and dashboard.

Natasha rushed to the vehicle. She quickly opened the door and tossed the dead driver to the cold ground. Then she got inside and sped off down the street. The incident happened so fast no one had heard or saw a thing.

Victor packed up his weapon and started his car. Seconds later he followed behind the large U-Haul truck. When they crossed the Benjamin Franklin Bridge, Vance's favorite crooked cop, John Carter, was waiting for them. Upon seeing the U-Haul, he sent Vance a text telling him the shipment was secured.

Inside the truck was over fifteen-hundred kilos of cocaine and a hundred kilos of heroin. It was the largest shipment that Vance had ever stolen from someone in one hit. This was a dream come true for Vance but an impending nightmare for Tito Vasquez.

LXII
HARLEM, NEW YORK

Tito and five of his most loyal men were talking inside of his private office. He had just received a major shipment of ten thousand kilos and was ready to flood the East Coast. His connects back in Colombia were depending on him. Tito was their major distributor for Canada and the East coast. Today's shipment was one of the largest to enter the Big Apple.

As they sat inside the office, the men never noticed the shadowy images on the security cameras. Unknowingly to them, a swarm of FBI, ATF and DEA agents had surrounded the entire warehouse. In less than thirty seconds the place was filled with armed agents. Three of Tito's men were shot and killed, as they tried to protect their boss as he ran away. However, Tito was eventually found hiding in the bathroom shower.

After Tito had been read his rights he was handcuffed and placed inside an FBI van and driven to the Federal Building. Tito had been charged under the 21 US Code 848 – Continuing a criminal enterprise. It was known as the CCE statute or the Kingpin statute. It was a federal law that targeted large-scale drug traffickers who were responsible for long-term elaborate drug conspiracies.

Tito knew that the sentence for a CCE conviction was a mandatory minimum twenty years' incarceration, a fine of two million, and the forfeiture of profits and any interest in the enterprise.

Tito was fucked and had been set up by someone on the inside. Realizing that he would never see the light of day, and he would serve the rest of his natural born life in a US Federal Penitentiary, his mind couldn't stop racing.

Once he arrived at The Federal Building, he was taken to a private room and surrounded by agents. His reign as King was now over. An agent walked up to him and stared into Tito's shocked eyes.

"You're looking at a life sentence. There's only one way you can help yourself now. Tell us everything we need to know and we can put in a good word with the prosecutor."

Tito looked up and said, "I have a life sentence to serve. Fuck y'all, take me to my cell!"

LXIII
ONE HOUR LATER
LIACOURAS CENTER

Vance looked at the incoming text message:
Tito Vazquez was apprehended in New York at 9:47 pm.
Thanks for your cooperation. We will be in touch soon.

Vance closed his cell phone and went back to watching the match. Bernard Hopkins was in a brutal battle with a formidable opponent. They were in round ten of the twelve round Championship fight. The event was broadcast live on HBO pay per view.

Biggie sat back in his seat watching Vance and Terry's every move. He was so focused on them he was unable to watch the fight.

The Philly crowd was brash and rowdy, cheering and clapping each time Bernard landed a solid punch. Their eyes were locked on Bernard's every move. And after a tough, exhausting, twelve round bout, Bernard Hopkins was the winner of a split decision victory.

Once the crowd had calmed down, Vance and Terry were nowhere in sight. They had managed to slip away into the crowd. Biggie was incensed, boiling with rage. He had his eyes on Vance and Terry the entire time, just to lose them in the crowd. Biggie, Zark, and Haze rushed around the venue looking in different directions. Neither found Vance or Terry.

Zeta was standing outside of the venue. She had received the text from Biggie, and she was armed and ready. Underneath her leather jacket was a 9mm with an attached silencer. If Zeta spotted Vance and Terry, she would shoot them without hesitation. They had brought so much pain, and misery to her life that she'd be honored to finish them off. Zeta wanted to end them tonight.

When Biggie and the rest of the crew came outside, they spotted Zeta. Biggie walked up to her and said, "You see anything?" Disappointedly she replied, "No, they must have left out another direction." "Damn," Biggie shouted. He had missed a chance to calm their storm, and he was furious.

LXIV
PENNSAUKEN, NJ

Rosa had been calling the driver of the U-Haul truck for the last forty-five minutes. The shipment was over an hour late, and she was very concerned. Over twenty million dollars' worth of cocaine was onboard the truck. When she called her cousin, Tito his phone calls went straight to his voicemail.

Rosa grabbed another cell phone from out of her purse. She logged into the vehicle's tracking application to locate its whereabouts. All of her trucks had the device implanted under the hood. Rosa watched as the small red dot on appeared on her phone's screen. The vehicle had moved all over North and West Philly. Immediately, she ordered her driver to get her to Philly as soon as possible.

Inside a tinted black S550 Mercedes Benz, Rosa and three of her goons sped off. Thirty minutes later they pulled up to the corner of Broad & Erie Avenue. They saw the large U-Haul truck parked on the side of Max's restaurant. The Mercedes pulled up and parked beside it. Everyone jumped out of the car pointing their weapons.

When one of the men looked inside the U-Haul, it was empty; with no sign of the driver. Rosa was on fire. Her face was blood red. This was the second time in just a few months that she lost an important drug shipment. Someone had inside information on the moves she was making.

As they headed back to Jersey, Rosa was in deep thought. She tried calling Tito's phone and the calls continued to go straight to voicemail. She had no answers and was skeptical when a private number came through her phone.

"Tito," Rosa said. "No, this is Paco. Tito was arrested a few hours ago at the warehouse. It's not looking good. I will be in touch when I have more info."

The phone went dead, and Rosa smiled. She usually smiled when she was her angriest. No one in the car knew what to say to Rosa because she could have easily pulled her pistol and blew one of their heads off. They were all silent as the crazed boss smiled and plotted her next move. Rosa needed to figure out what the hell was going on!

LXV
BALA CYNWYD, PA

Vance pulled the black Range Rover in the back of his beautiful home. He then opened the double car garage and parked inside. Vance walked into his home and turned on the lights in the kitchen. The living room was pitch black when he entered. When Vance turned the lights on he was startled to see his daughter, Queen, sitting on the sofa in the dark.

"You scared the hell out of me," Vance shouted. He noticed the severe expression on Queen's face. "What's wrong? Your new husband fucked up already," he joked. Queen stood up from the sofa and walked over to her father. Queen stared straight into her father's eyes and said, "No, me and my husband are doing just fine. In fact, he's outside in the car waiting for me."

"Then what is it? Why do you look so serious," he asked. Queen continued to stare into her father's eyes and then she cleared her throat. "Why did you kill my mother? Why did you poison her?"

Vance was shocked at what he was hearing. Before he could conjure up a lie, Queen interrupted him. "I know you did it so don't lie to me! You never read her journal. She wrote everything down in there. I know what you did to her. She even wrote down that you're a snitch who works for the FEDS. I know it all now! All of your secrets! All about those two FBI Agents who are always around! You poisoned my mother, and you are a fucking snitch! The one thing that you always despised, that's what you are! Why Daddy!!! Why

Daddy!!! Why did you do it!!! I don't even know you anymore! Who are you?!?"

As Queen venting out her frustration, Vance stood silently. Her words had penetrated his soul. He had never wanted anyone to learn of his darkest secret. For years, it had haunted him. Being a snitch wasn't something he set out to be. When he got into the game he was as ruthless as anyone, but being behind bars just wasn't for him. He knew that he could only enjoy his life in the game if he never had to serve time. When he was presented with his get-out-of-jail card, he knew exactly what he had to do to keep it.

As Queen yelled and cried out, all her frustration Vance didn't know what to do. His mind began to wander to a time before it all went wrong...

LXVI
TWENTY-ONE YEARS AGO
WEST PHILLY

The gray Infiniti Q45 pulled up and parked on the corner of 43RD & Lancaster Avenue. Parked on the opposite side of the street was a tinted black Lexus. Face and his partner Reese were inside. Vance got out of his car and ran across the street. When he opened the back door and sat down inside, he saw the small backpack laying on the floor.

"That's the five keez you asked for," Reese told him. Vance took out a small brown bag, filled with cash from inside his leather jacket. He passed the bag of money to Reese and said, "That's every penny I owe Y'all."

Face watched but didn't say a single word. Vance had always been a good customer, but there was something about his character Face didn't like. Face knew Vance was the type of man that wasn't loyal to anything but his money. He despised men like Vance because he knew those kinds of men could never be trusted. That's why he rarely spoke when he was in his presence.

After Vance grabbed the backpack and got out of the car, Face and Reese sped off down the street.
"You really don't like him, huh?"
"Not at all. I feel like he's the type of guy that will tell on his own mother if it could keep him out of jail. He talks too fast and never listens. You have to watch men like that."
"Well so far so good. He spends a lot of money with us," Reese said, as he pulled his car onto Girard Avenue.

"If he ever crosses me I'm going to make sure he disappears, along with his stripper girlfriend and their little daughter," Face said.

ONE HOUR LATER

Vance pulled his car into the Friday's parking lot on City Line Avenue. He got out of his car and walked over to the nearby Holiday Inn Hotel. He walked through the lobby and made his way to the 4th floor. With his backpack filled with five kilos-four of them pure cocaine and one, a kilo of crack-Vance rushed to room 412. He knocked on the door and was immediately let into the room.

Two Jamaican drug dealers were inside. Sammy V and Chucky were their names. For the last six months, Vance had been selling them cocaine and guns.

Vance sat down and opened the backpack. He took out the five kilos and said, "Thirty a piece. This is the best coke you'll ever get in Philly. It ain't been touched or stepped on." Sammy V and Chucky tested the product. Vance watched as the two Jamaicans snorted a line of coke with a straw.

"Good shit Vance," Chucky said. Sammy V then grabbed a small briefcase from under the bed and opened it. Inside the briefcase was one-hundred-fifty thousand dollars in cash. Vance's eyes lit up with delight. He had only paid fifteen-thousand a kilo, and with the sell, he was doubling his money.

Vance closed the briefcase and stood up. As he shook the men's hands, the bathroom door burst open. Two armed FBI Agents rushed into the room, and two more agents rushed through the front door. They slammed Vance and the two Jamaicans to the floor, as they read the drug dealers their rights.

Thirty minutes later, Vance was at the Federal Building downtown. Inside a medium sized room, he was being interrogated by the two FBI Agents. Vance was nervous and sweating profusely.

"I don't know shit! And I ain't snitching on nobody," Vance said. One of the agents grabbed Vance by his collar. "You think this is a damn game! If you don't tell us what we want to know you're never getting out of jail!" he shouted. "Get Charles and Victor," he told his partner.

A few moments later The Agent walked back into the room with two black men. "Remember these two men Vance," The Agent asked. Vance was shocked. All he could do was shake his head in disbelief.

"This is Special Agent Victor Jackson and his partner Charles Parrish. You know them as Sammy V and Chucky. We have over six months of direct buys on the wiretaps. That's more than enough for a life sentence with no chance of parole tough guy!"

The two black agents walked out of the room, and Vance knew he was fucked. "What is it that Y'all want from me," Vance said. "We want it all! We want to know everything you know that's going on in the streets. We need to know every major player and the moves they make. We want you to help us bring them all down! If you cooperate and work with us, you will never spend one day inside of a prison. We will let the Federal Prosecutor know that you're on our side. If you give us what we need we will have you placed in the Federal Witness Protection program, with your family," The Agent said.

"Why me," Vance asked. "Because you're very connected to the streets. You're a major player in Philly, and we need you. Now you need us," the Agent replied. "So who do Y'all want," Vance said. "Everybody! Every major drug dealer in Philly, Jersey, and Delaware! We want Al Cash, Duke, and Jimmy, and most importantly we want you to help us get Face."

"Face and Reese," Vance asked. "Yes, that Face," the Agent said. "What's wrong you scared of him?" Vance looked at both agents with a somber expression.

"Face is on another level. He's a legend in Philly," Vance said. "Are you with us or not Mr. Lewis? If you're not willing to cooperate with us then we will have you escorted to the Federal Detention Center, and we will see you at your trial," the Agent threatened.

"I'm in," Vance whispered. The agent opened the door and called a woman inside the room. In walked a petite, Caucasian woman with two sheets of paper in her hand. She laid them down in front of Vance, and said, "Hi Mr. Lewis I'm the Special Prosecutor for the Eastern District of Pennsylvania. These documents state your willingness to become an informant for the United States government. You will now report to your assigned Agents. You will also be given a Federal Probation Officer. You'll need to submit weekly urine and drug tests. Which you need to pass. Please read over these form and sign where indicated."

Vance signed on the dotted line and in that moment he had become the one thing he despised, A SNITCH!

LXVII
BALA CYNWYD, PA

"You're a murderer and a fucking snitch! I hate you," Queen continue to shout. Vance stood there in silence. His daughter had learned that not only was he a snitch, but he was responsible for her mother's death. He thought about saying sorry. He thought about telling her he wished he could change the past, but no words came out of his mouth. Vance could only watch as his outraged child scolded him.

Queen was hurt beyond words and there was nothing he could say to erase the pain and anguish she was living with.

Queen took two steps back and suddenly pulled out a loaded 9mm. She pointed her gun at her father's head and said, "I hate you! I hate everything that you stand for! I hate you for killing my mother! Why did you do it? Because she found out your secret?"

"Put that damn gun down Queen," Vance demanded. "Fuck you," she yelled.

Suddenly the front door opened, and King walked in. After hearing the commotion, he decided to see what was going on. Vance and King stared at one another, trying to piece the puzzle together.

"You brought my enemy to my house," Vance snapped. "This is your father," King yelled. Queen was confused.

"Vance is your dad? He's the man that's trying to kill me," King shouted. "King is your husband? You married my fuckin enemy! Are you serious," Vance shouted back.

In the midst of all the commotion Vance and King both pulled out their weapons. Vance had his .40 caliber pointed at King. King had his .45 caliber pointed at Vance, and Queen had her 9mm aimed at Vance's head.

"You know my father," she asked. "Yes, I've known him for years! He wants my empire, and he's been trying to take me and my crew out," King said. "Fuck you, you coward! You don't deserve a damn thing! Everyone knows that your cousin passed you a torch that's too big to carry," Vance shouted. "Queen, kill this motherfucker," Vance demanded. "Fuck no, you snitch ass murderer," Queen cried.

For a moment, the room froze. The unlikeliness of this situation was rarer than someone winning a mega-million lottery. Guns were pointed at everyone, but no one pulled the trigger.

"Kill this motherfucker Queen! Then I will tell you everything you need to know," Vance said. "You're my father, but he is my KING," Queen replied.

Before Vance could say another word a silent bullet burst through the living room window, striking Vance in the side of his throat. Blood gushed from his neck as he grabbed his throat, struggling to breathe. He fell to the floor trying to call out for help.

Queen and King ducked and ran for cover as a barrage of bullets started flying through the house. Suddenly, the shooting had ceased, and they heard the sound of a car speeding away.

"Let's get the Fuck out of here," King told Queen. "Hold up," Queen said. She then walked over to her dying father and said, "Die slow you snitch bastard!" Vance lay there clinging to consciousness and barely able to move.

King and Queen rushed out of the door and sped off in their car. As Vance lay there bleeding profusely, he struggled to get into his pants pocket. Managing to get his cell phone he dialed the last number he had called.

"Hello, Babe. Hello? Hello, Vance are you okay?" Unable to speak Vance dropped the phone as his pain overwhelmed him. "Hello? Baby are you okay? Hello? Vance, answer me," the woman continued to cry out.

LXVIII
MOMENTS LATER

A dark blue Ford Escort pulled behind the Burger King and parked. "We did it," Plex yelled out. "I got that motherfucker! I shot him right in the head! That's what happens when you fuck with mines!"

Bobby sat behind the wheel watching as his animated friend celebrated. Plex had finally killed the man who was responsible for murdering his wife. Bobby knew that Plex couldn't have rested until he killed Vance. Bobby was glad that it was now all over because searching for Vance had been a tedious and tiresome task.

It was pure luck that had led Plex to Vance. His youngest daughter, Kristen, had posted a picture of their house on Instagram. She didn't think to hide the address and Plex was already familiar with the area. So once he saw the photo, it was just the luck he needed to get his revenge. His own child had led to his demise and Plex could think of no better irony. Plex began to cry as Bobby pulled off down the street. Bobby was ready to drop his friend off because tonight he needed to go home and hug his wife. He had spent too many nights away from the woman he loved trying to help Plex. And after this tragedy, he didn't want to spend another moment away from his woman.

LXIX
THIRTY-FIVE MINUTES LATER

"Vance is your father? I still can't believe it," King said. "I told you I grew up in and around the drug game," Queen said, as King drove on. "But you never said your father was Vance Lewis. What a small fuckin world," King said, shaking his head in disbelief. "I wonder who was shooting at him. Someone wanted him dead," King said. "Yeah, someone else he probably fucked over," Queen replied.

King pulled up and parked outside of his City Line Avenue apartment. He was still very shaken up about how things had unfolded, and the discovery of Queen's biological father was unbelievable.

Under a bright fall moon, they exited their vehicle and walked towards the apartment.

"So Babe, what were you talking about when you called your father a snitch?" Before Queen could respond a shadowy figure emerged from behind a tree aiming a loaded .38 caliber pistol. The individual pulled the trigger twice, hitting King in the stomach.

King fell to the cold ground as the being ran off. Queen had been totally caught off guard and before she could react King was laying on the ground bleeding. She screamed out as loud as she could.

"Somebody call an ambulance!!! Someone call an ambulance!!! HELP ME! HELP ME! PLEASE," Queen continued to cry out. "Baby don't die; Baby don't die on me!! Don't die on me, PLEASE!!!"

It seemed like an eternity as Queen huddled on the ground with King, crying out for help. Finally, an ambulance arrived and quickly placed King inside. Queen entered the ambulance, and she was numb. He lover had just been shot in front of her, and his life was slipping away. All she could do was cry and pray. King's life was now in the hands of his Maker.

FIFTEEN MINUTES LATER
GERMANTOWN

Sofie rushed into her apartment and sat down on the sofa. She was nervous and shaking uncontrollably. She had just shot the man who had caused her to endure a separation from her lover. For the first time in months, Sofie had felt some relief. Her plan had gone perfectly.

Sofie knew it was now best for her to get out of town. She had an older sister in Baltimore, so after packing up a suitcase she headed to the 30th Street Train Station. Sofie knew if Queen had gotten any intuition that she shot King, her life was now in danger. She needed to hide, and she had no reasons to stay in Philly. Sofia was going to leave and never look back.

LXX
TWO DAYS LATER

Inside the Roxborough Memorial Hospital, located in Bala Cynwyd, Pennsylvania, Vance lay down in his hospital bed. He had been shot in the neck. Luckily, the bullet missed his main carotid artery by a mere centimeter. If the bullet had hit the carotid artery, it would've stopped his blood supply to his brain and Vance would've died.

Thankfully, JoAnn rushed to him to see what was wrong. Had she assumed it was an accidental call, Vance would've bled out or choked on his own blood.

Vance was unable to talk. The doctors told him it would be a while before he could get his voice back, and for now, they wanted him to rest. Once he was cleared to begin rehab, they were sure he'd be speaking in just a few weeks. Until then he was given a small yellow notepad and pen to communicate.

Vance was surrounded by his closest family and friends. Victor, Natasha, JoAnn, Terry, and his young daughter Kristen and her mother. Rosa and one of her goons had also come for a visit.

Rosa walked over to Vance and whispered in his ear, "Tell me who did this to you." Vance grabbed his pen and pad and started writing something down. When he finished, he folded up the paper and handed it to Rosa.

Rosa wanted to tell Vance about her cousin Tito, and the robbery of her shipments but she didn't wish to speak out of term. Vance had his family there, and she figured they could talk once he was better.

Rosa kissed Vance on the cheek and said, "Get well soon. We will talk when you're feeling better, and your voice is stronger." Then Rosa and her goon said their goodbyes and walked out of the room.

Once Rosa got into her waiting Mercedes and was comfortably in her seat, she took out the piece of paper Vance gave her. Once she unfolded it she started to read the message Vance had written down:

My daughter Queen set me up, and she shot me. I need you to kill that bitch!

LXXI
UNIVERSITY OF PENNSYLVANIA HOSPITAL

For two days King had been laying in the ICU in critical condition. The doctors had done all they could do to save his life, and now it was up to him to pull through. The bullets had damaged his colon, pancreas, and kidney; and there was severe blood loss.

As he lay in a coma, Queen never left his side. His entire crew and bodyguard had been waiting in the visitor's room, each preparing to hear the worst.

Queen sat by his side looking at all the IVs attached to his arms and the small thin tube strapped to his mouth. A little heart monitor kept track of his heart rate, blood pressure, and pulse. Queen hadn't slept in two days, and her face was drained from worry.

Queen knew who had shot King. The shadowy figure's face was not seen, but her body was. Queen and Sofie were lovers. There wasn't a part of Sofie's body Queen couldn't recognize. Queen had seen Sofie's physique in and out of clothing. On the ride to the hospital, Queen knew Sofie was the gunman. Queen gave all her attention to her husband because he needed her most. She didn't have time to plot her revenge, but as soon as King recovered she'd deal with Sofie and make her pay. That was a promise.

Suddenly the room door opened, and Face and Quincy walked inside. Queen was very surprised to see him.

"I talked to the doctor, and he said it's nothing more they could. We have to wait and see what happens," Face said to Queen.

Face looked at his younger cousin and was instantly saddened. He began to blame himself for not stepping in. He was hurt, and his rage started to heat up.

Face walked over and stared at King's face. He wouldn't allow himself to shed a tear. Already, in the privacy of his home, Face had gotten down on his knees and begged God to spare King's life.

Face leaned down and put his mouth to King's ear. "Real niggas don't die! Get through this and the world will be yours. God ain't finished with you yet. There's so much more for you to live for. Dying is not what we do." With that said, Face and Quincy walked out of the room.

After they had left the room, Queen grabbed King's hand and placed it on her stomach. She knew King could feel her presence and that he could hear her words.

"Our Prince needs his King and so do I. Fight Babe, and come back to us," Queen said, as the tears rolled down her cheeks.

COMING SOON

KING II

LAUGH NOW/ DIE LATER

JIMMY DASAINT

COMING SOON

DASAINT ENT PRESENTS

THE RISE OF A DYNASTY

JIMMY DASAINT

DASAINT ENTERTAINMENT ORDER FORM

Please visit www.dasaintentertainment.com to place online orders.

You can also fill out this form and send it to:

DASAINT ENTERTAINMENT
PO BOX 97
BALA CYNWYD, PA 19004

TITLE	PRICE	QTY
BLACK SCARFACE	$15.00	_____
BLACK SCARFACE II	$15.00	_____
BLACK SCARFACE III	$15.00	_____
BLACK SCARFACE IV	$15.00	_____
DOC	$15.00	_____
KING	$15.00	_____
YOUNG RICH & DANGEROUS	$15.00	_____
WHAT EVERY WOMAN WANTS	$15.00	_____
THE UNDERWORLD	$15.00	_____
A ROSE AMONG THORNS	$15.00	_____
A ROSE AMONG THORNS II	$15.00	_____
CONTRACT KILLER	$15.00	_____
MONEY DESIRES & REGRETS	$15.00	_____
ON EVERYTHING I LOVE	$15.00	_____
WHO	$15.00	_____
AIN'T NO SUNSHINE	$15.00	_____
SEX SLAVE	$15.00	_____
THE DARKEST CORNER	$15.00	_____
KILLADELPHIA	$15.00	_____

Make Checks or Money Orders payable to:
DASAINT ENTERTAINMENT

NAME: _____

ADDRESS: _____

_____

CITY: _____ STATE: _____
ZIP: _____ PHONE: _____

PRISON ID NUMBER_____

$3.50 per item for Shipping and Handling
($4.95 per item for Expedited Shipping)

WE SHIP TO PRISONS!!!

DEDICATION

First I want to thank God for getting me through my ten years of darkness, and leading me back into the light. I dedicate this book to all my fallen comrades that lie in the grave, To my brothers and sisters in state and federal prison systems, To my brother, Sean "Shiz" Mathis, I miss you, and you will always be in my heart, To Georgie, Mark, Man, Trump, Lil Rob, my best friend 4 life Wallace "Duke" Gray, my Homies; Cheeze, Rob Hennigan, Big Nas, Sport, Khan Jamal, and Vance, it's all love. To my sisters, Dawn, Tammy, and Tanya; I love you. To my mother Belinda Mathis and Mr. Nate, you two have been nothing but an everlasting blessing to me. To Tiona Brown, I want to thank you for having my back always. To my sons, Jaiden Prince Mathis, Nigel, and Marquise, I love you all. To Katrina Henderson, thank you. To the Brown/Cannon family I thank you for always attending my events and giving me constant support. Erica Willis and your entire family, thanks for your support. To all of the Mathis family, Joyce, Gal, Annie, Sweet Pea, Zark, China, Sterling, Bam, Aunt Candi, and Uncle Larry, I thank you for all of your support.

To my West Philly Hood 42nd & 43rd Street, to my rap group I.C.H., to my mentor and good friend, Freeway Rick Ross, I salute you. To my city of Philadelphia (the most talented but hated on city in America), I couldn't ask to be from a better place.

A very special dedication to one of my biggest fans and a true friend, Marrion "Myrt" Henderson, I will always miss you.

74415624R00117

Made in the USA
Middletown, DE
24 May 2018